COMPLICATIONS ON ICE

COMPLICATIONS ON ICE

BOYS OF WINTER #3

S.R. GREY

This is a work of fiction. Names, characters, places, and incidents are products of the author's imagination or are used fictitiously and are not considered to be real. Any resemblance to actual events, locales, organizations, or persons, living or dead, is entirely coincidental.

Complications on Ice (Boys of Winter #3)
Copyright © 2017 by S.R. Grey

ISBN-10: 0-9979749-5-8
ISBN-13: 978-0-9979749-5-9

Editors: Hot Tree Editing
Proofreader: Deaton Author Services
Cover Photographer: CJC Photography
Model: Alex Neff
Cover Design: Najla Qamber
Interior Design and Formatting: by:
www.emtippettsbookdesigns.com

OTHER BOOKS BY
S.R. GREY

Boys of Winter series
Destiny on Ice
Resistance on Ice
Complications on Ice

Judge Me Not series
I Stand Before You
Never Doubt Me
Just Let Me Love You
The After of Us

Inevitability duology
Inevitable Detour
Inevitable Circumstances

Promises series
Tomorrow's Lies
Today's Promises

A Harbour Falls Mystery trilogy
Harbour Falls
Willow Point
Wickingham Way

Laid Bare novella series
Exposed: Laid Bare 1
Unveiled: Laid Bare 2
Spellbound: Laid Bare 3
Sacrifice: Laid Bare 4

OH, BABY

ELIZA

"Eliza? Eliza?" A light knock on my bedroom door roused me from the nap I was sneaking in. "Are you up?"

Ah, I was now. But I had to smile. My mother, bless her soul, she'd been a godsend.

"Yes, Mom," I replied. "I'm wide awake in here." *Small lie.*

"Oh, good, honey." I heard her sigh. "'Cause we need to leave real soon. Our flight leaves at two. And you know for a fact, since you're wide awake and all"—she cleared her throat, onto me—"that it's already half past eleven."

Uh-oh, busted. And was it really after eleven?

I checked my phone, and it sure was.

Time to get my ass in gear.

Rolling onto my back, I yelled, "I'll be out in a minute." *Or two.*

More like three…

Or four…

Or more…

See, getting out of bed required energy, something I'd been sorely lacking lately. To be honest, I'd never felt more mentally or physically exhausted than I had these past several weeks.

Not *ever* in my life.

But my life had changed.

That's why it'd been a good thing my mom had stayed on at my apartment to help me out. The before was easy, it was the now that was hard.

How do women do this by themselves? I thought.

"Damned if I know," I murmured as I stared up at a mural someone had painted on the ceiling long before I'd ever lived here.

Sunshine, an arid desert, a cactus in full bloom. All rendered in bright, vivid colors.

These were things I'd see real soon, as in real life, not simply as images painted in watercolor on a ceiling.

Damn, I couldn't believe I was heading back to Las Vegas after all this time out on my own. That's what this upcoming flight was about. A few hours from now, I'd start a new chapter in my life.

"Yet *another* new chapter," I breathed out.

So much had changed in such a short period of time. Some days it felt like my head might spin right the hell off my neck.

Wow, what an image. Exhaustion can do that to you, though.

Hell with that. It was high time I woke the hell up, put on my big girl panties, and let go of the past. I vowed right then and there to face the future with a smile.

But I needed motivation, something to get me on track.

Glancing around the mostly-empty room, I searched for inspiration. And then, amid the barrenness, I saw it. The motivation I sought was right there in a framed photo I'd left on the wall. Ironically, or maybe fortuitously, it was the only thing I'd not packed up and shipped off earlier in the week.

The photo was something my dad had sent me. It was of him and the team he coached, the Las Vegas Wolves, celebrating their recent Stanley Cup win.

I liked that picture. I liked it a lot. That's why I'd hung it on the wall right across from my bed. It was proof of how believing in yourself, whether individually or as part of a team, could lead to winning it all.

But there was another reason why I'd held onto the picture. It had to do with the guy front and center. He, like the rest of the team, was still in his gear, sans helmet.

Having just won the Stanley Cup, half the team, including him, was lying on the ice. But *he* stood out. His wild dark blond hair and his big hands grasping hockey's Holy Grail, he just struck me as a guy who really enjoyed life. His smile seemed so genuine, his happiness, palpable.

Not to mention, he was *hot.*

I had a weakness for hockey players, so in three seconds flat, I was grabbing up my phone, forgetting about Mom outside my door, and looking him up.

Why hadn't I done this sooner? I guess because I was "asleep." No more.

"Number twenty-nine," I read aloud as I skimmed his bio on the Wolves's website. "Benjamin Perry, but he goes by Benny. A forward, plays left wing."

I lowered my phone and smiled. Oh, I had a plan. And Benny

Perry had better watch out.

I had a new crush, just like that. Impulsivity, I lived by it.

Pursuing this Perry dude wouldn't be easy, though. I'd have to be sly about it, especially around my hockey coach dad. After all that had recently transpired in my life, he'd taken to implementing preemptive measures designed to keep me far, far away from his players. He'd made sure I knew about it, too.

Just last week, when we were on the phone, he oh-so-cheerily informed me he'd warned each and every one of the Wolves to stay the hell away from me.

"Why would you do something crazy like that?" I demanded to know.

"Eliza,"—I imagined him shaking his head—"do you really need to ask that question?"

Okay, he had me there.

"Still, isn't a warning to the players a bit extreme?" I threw out.

"I don't think so, honey. Not after what all has happened." His voice ticked up an octave when, after a pause, he added, "And especially not when you continue to refuse to tell me *or* your mother who the hell—"

I knew where that was headed, and I nipped it in the bud quickly. "That's enough, Dad."

On this, I was set.

"I see you're still avoiding the whole subject," he groused.

"Yes, yes I am."

He huffed then, and in a softer tone, I tried to reason with him. "Dad, look, I'm sorry, okay? I didn't mean to snap at you. I just haven't been myself lately."

"S'okay, Eliza."

"Does that mean we can *please* let this go?" He didn't know I *had* to avoid this topic.

He agreed, at last, but slipped into Strict Dad mode, his go-to for handling stress.

"You just better behave yourself while you're living under my roof, young lady. If you do, I'll never push for a name."

Good, because he wasn't getting one.

Shit, it was clear now that dating was going to be tricky. And Wolves players were out.

My new life was put in perspective after that call. I would be stuck living with my dad's rules. At least most of my Georgetown credits had transferred to UNLV, where I'd soon be matriculating. I couldn't wait to start classes in the fall. If I could still graduate by spring, I'd have my own place by next summer.

Even so, I'd never have back the life I once knew.

"I mean it, Eliza." Mom went crazy on the door then, her patience worn thin. "I've been standing out here for ten minutes. You need to get your butt up *now*."

"I told you I *am* up," I yelled, throwing off the covers.

"Look, I realize you're exhausted"—*ha, understatement of the year*—"but I need you dressed and ready. The taxi's on its way, and if we're not ready to roll the driver *will* leave. This is DC, after all."

I didn't reply, and she continued, "The next flight out to Las Vegas isn't till almost midnight, Eliza. And you know as well as I do that we can't sit around in an airport for hours on end with a b—"

"All right, okay." I threw my legs over the side of the bed. "I'm up, I'm really up this time."

I stood to back up my words, but, whoa, my legs protested. It felt like someone had poured cement down them. I was *that* damn tired.

Mom, meanwhile, was finally done.

"That's it." I heard her mumble. "I'm going in."

The door swung open, but I didn't put up a fuss. Her coming in was for the best. She'd make sure my cement legs didn't win out and send me crawling back to bed.

"Hey, Mom." I waved.

Running her hand through her strawberry-blonde hair, same color as mine, she sighed. "Good, you really are up."

Rolling my eyes, and again, due to exhaustion creeping back in, I snapped, "I'm not as irresponsible as you and Dad think I am."

All that ruminating on my dad's ban on hockey players had made me an irritated bitch.

Mom blew out a breath and said softly, "Sweetheart, I don't think that about you."

She was trying to make me feel better, but it wasn't her I needed reassurance from.

"Dad thinks I am," I mumbled.

"Oh, sweetie, he'll come around. This is all just hard for him. You've been his little girl forever, you know?"

I had to remind her, "I'm not a child, Mom. I'm twenty-one. Not to mention..." I gave her a do-we-need-to-review-recent-events glare. "...my new life says for sure I'm an adult."

She sat down on the edge of the bed, and I joined her. "Honey, come here."

She pulled me in for a hug, and I felt a million times better.

"Thanks for always being here for me," I murmured into her sweet-smelling hair. "You came through when no one else had the time."

"Always, Eliza," she said. "I'll always have time for you."

"You're the best," I whispered. "I love you, Mom."

"I love you, too, honey." Leaning back, she shook her head. "It's also my duty to make sure you don't go out in public dressed like that."

"Huh?"

She nodded to my attire, or lack thereof.

"Oh, crap, you're right." I was wearing nothing but panties and an old, faded gray tee, making me surmise, "I guess pants might be a good idea."

"You think?"

"Ha-ha, Mom."

I retrieved the yoga pants I'd peeled off earlier and slipped them on, smiling like *ta-da*.

Mom still looked worried.

"What's wrong now?" I asked, scanning down to my feet. *That must be it.* "I'll put on shoes before we leave," I promised.

"Shoes aren't the problem, Eliza."

"They aren't?"

"Um, no."

She wasn't giving my shoeless feet a second thought; she was staring at my chest.

"What are you looking at—?"

Softly, she said, "I think you need to change your shirt. Or at least put on some kind of cover-up."

I took a better look—damn exhaustion!—and finally saw the problem. "Oh, shit, I'm leaking!"

Just then, like someone knew the shake shack—me—was open for business, a baby began to cry.

My baby.

"Ava," I murmured.

The powerful emotions I felt for my barely eight-week-old daughter sometimes overwhelmed me.

"She must be hungry," I added dreamily.

Yes, I was a little bit in awe of the gorgeous little girl in the next room. I just couldn't freaking believe she was really mine.

"She's been sleeping for a while," Mom said, pulling me from my wandering thoughts. "Like someone else I know."

"Cute, Mom."

I left the room then to feed my daughter before the taxi arrived. As I fed baby Ava, I thought about how this was really the end of my old life. Off to Las Vegas we were going. That was okay. It was time to move forward. No more sheltering up in the apartment with my mom and my baby. It was time to get back to the real world for all of us. Only problem was there'd be questions—*lots* of questions. Ones I couldn't answer, for a multitude of reasons.

But then I had an idea—if I kept Ava a secret, no one would have anything to ask. There was no need to broadcast *why* I was returning to Las Vegas, right? I didn't have to explain everything right away.

I looked down at my daughter. "We should settle in first. Right, Ava? Then we can worry about everything else later."

Ava didn't care one way or the other, so I got back to thinking it through on my own. There was a lot more to think about, too. Because when I *did* get around to telling the world about my daughter, there was a huge secret I'd still have to keep.

I'd stupidly made an agreement with Ava's father.

Part one was I could live anywhere I wanted *and* he'd continue to pay the child support we'd agreed upon, but Ava was to retain *my* last name—the one I'd had to put on the birth certificate, Townsend. Not his.

That really burned me.

Even after the paternity test he'd demanded, the very one that proved he was definitely her dad, the jerk still wanted to keep his name off any and all public records. I was pretty much ordered *by* him to *keep* him a secret. All because he didn't want the world to know he, a professional hockey player, had fathered a child. He claimed it could legit damage his up-and-coming career and endorsement deals.

That was bullshit.

He wasn't some clean-cut sweetheart of a guy. He was simply trying to maintain his carefree, playboy lifestyle.

He was a major asshole like that.

Too bad I hadn't realized it before I slept with him.

But I was blind. And sleep with him I did, more than once.

My parents didn't know *who* I'd messed around with, but I'd let it slip once that Ava's dad was a hockey player. Bad move on my part. That was what kicked off my dad's obsession with keeping me away from *all* hockey players.

Too bad I also had to keep my dad away from something—the truth. I was afraid of what would happen if I didn't. But crap, it wasn't going to be an easy task. Not when Ava's father played for a team that played the Wolves several times a season.

And that new season started real soon. Training camp was only six weeks away, for heaven's sake.

So, yeah, no, keeping all these secrets was going to be a challenge.

"It probably won't end well," I murmured.

Truer words could not have been spoken.

2

A BIGGER PROBLEM THAN A CHOCOLATE-FROSTED DONUT

BENNY

"Grant me the strength to accept the things I cannot change, the courage to change the things I can, and the wisdom to know the difference."

Every time I uttered those words, I was reminded I wasn't simply Benjamin "Benny" Perry, premier left winger for the Las Vegas Wolves. I was also a twenty-nine-year-old former substance abuser.

That former part was important, and I worked on it every single day. Management and my teammates liked to think I'd changed completely, that I was long done with my partying ways of the past. I was, but only because I attended meetings like the one that had just wrapped up.

The fact was, every fucking day of staying clean and sober took as much effort, if not more so, as playing good hockey.

Some days were a breeze, and some days were…not.

Today was one of the latter. It started out rough, beginning with when I woke up at dawn in bed with a random puck bunny. No alcohol or drugs were involved. I was just a dog, battling the only vice I'd not yet conquered—easy sex. It was the one addiction I couldn't quite beat. Well, the only one if you didn't count my weakness for donuts. If you counted that, then there were two.

I could live with the donut problem. It wasn't that bad. Besides, I wasn't giving up donuts for anything. Our team-mandated player diet, which I'd soon be adhering to, would have to allow for some wiggle room this season.

That's why I felt okay about stopping for a donut on the way to this meeting. *It was an emergency, damn it.* Or so I told myself. I was soon convinced I *needed* a big chocolate-frosted donut to soothe my puck bunny woes.

It helped, but what I'd really needed was this meeting. I felt better already having just talked things out. Not that I'd confessed any major details of my little indiscretion. I'd simply spoken of challenges in general. Still, I felt good now. I always did after sharing shit with people like me.

The people in this particular group were *all* like me. As in, everyone in attendance that morning in the basement of a Las Vegas church on the outskirts of town was either a former, or present-day, athlete who was battling an addiction.

I happened to fall into the "present-day" category. I was in the prime of my hockey career, having just won the motherfucking Stanley Cup. That was great, but winning it all didn't make everything rosy. I'd learned long ago that life was not perfect, even when it seemed it should be.

Every man in the room that morning knew that.

That's why we'd started our little group. This church really was our haven. And these meetings provided a place where we all understood one another on a level no one else ever really could.

That bond was essential for our success. We felt comfortable calling each other out and sifting through the BS. In other words, we could be ourselves.

The chair creaked beneath me as I yawned and stretched. In fact, a bunch of chairs murmured the same dissent as other guys did the same. The cheap-ass things were nothing but folding pieces of thin metal crap. They hadn't been designed to hold men as big and muscular as the ones in the room.

Speaking of muscles, mine were screaming for a good massage. Good thing preseason had started. I could schedule one at any time. I'd gone really hard at practice this morning and I was feeling it now. The pain was worth it. After dealing with all my mixed-up feelings regarding the random sex with the stranger, I'd needed that release.

A bunch of guys stood then, including me, but we remained in the circle of chairs. There were twelve of us in all who met regularly, and we enjoyed sticking around afterward to bullshit about this or that.

Then there was the coffee and donuts in the back.

That right there kept me around.

I made a beeline for the sugar and caffeine, and after pouring a coffee so black it looked like tar, I added in some sweetener, and then grabbed a heavily chocolate-frosted donut from the tray.

As I savored the first gooey bite, a guy bigger than me—and I was six feet two, so that was really saying something—strode up and handed me a napkin.

"Here, Perry. No need to be a pig about things."

Graham Tettersaw, the giant next to me, smirked as I shot him the finger.

Too late, I thought, *you should have seen me last night. The things I did to that girl…*

"I have to say," he went on, nodding to the donut. "That's some heavy-duty sugar consumption, even for you. I know it's only training camp, but doesn't the regular season start soon?"

"It does indeed, Graham," I mumbled as I swallowed.

"Maybe you ought to be laying off the sweets, then?"

I chortled, "What are you, my goddamn mother?"

He laughed. "You clearly need some kind of guidance. So sure, I can stand in for good 'ole mom if needed."

"You're such a prick," I shot back.

Our banter was all in good fun. Graham took a special joy in giving me a hard time. And I enjoyed giving it right the fuck back to him. He was an athlete, like me, an ex-football star. More importantly, Graham was my sponsor. I relied on him. I especially had in the early days of staying sober, those times when I couldn't even attend events where alcohol was being served. I'd also discovered, over the past year, Graham Tettersaw was a true stand-up guy.

He used to play ball for the Phoenix Cardinals. Quarterback, till he blew out his knee. After he was cut from the team, he developed a nasty painkiller addiction.

That's what landed him in rehab…and why he was here today.

But Graham was clean going on three years now. He strongly believed in paying it forward. That's why he became a sponsor.

He was also looking to play ball again, as I'd recently learned.

"Maybe," he said when I caught him running drills and asked if he was looking to get back in the game.

There were no maybe about it, far as I could see. He'd been working out for months and had as good a chance as anyone at making a comeback. Dude was strong as an ox and still had the right moves. It wouldn't be easy, though. Graham had just turned thirty and had been away from playing pro ball since getting hurt.

If anyone could do it, my money was on him. He was a persistent bastard, if nothing else. As demonstrated when he started riding me when I picked up another donut.

The other guys had descended on the table and the chocolate-frosted ones were going like hotcakes, so I'd acted fast.

"Aw, fuck you, man." I laughed, pointing my new donut at Graham. "Do you ever stop?"

Apparently not, since, suppressing a grin, he volleyed back, "You're gonna get fat, lose your speed. Then you'll get demoted to the goon line and be whining like a baby."

From around a mouthful of dough, I cursed him out.

After I swallowed, I informed him, "The season doesn't start till October, dick. There's plenty of time to indulge."

"Hmm, I don't know what calendar you're looking at, but mine shows that's only two weeks away." Graham nodded to the donut—or rather to what was left of it. "I wonder what the team nutritionist will have to say about your massive donut habit."

"She'll say it's fine if I indulge only once in a while."

"She will, huh?"

"Yep, she will."

I polished off the donut and licked my fingers clean. I guess I looked guilty about more than donuts since Graham raised a brow.

"You sure we're only talking about donuts here?" he queried.

Since indulge-once-in-a-while was pretty much how I'd justified last night's sexcapade, I almost came clean. But then I worried we'd get into the *whys* of what I'd done, and I just didn't feel like addressing those yet.

Sheepishly, I simply replied, "Yeah, I'm sure."

Clapping me on the back, Graham grabbed a donut for himself.

"Hey," he said, "you know I'm just fucking with you, huh? I know you've been doing really well."

Blowing shit off was sometimes Graham's way of drilling down to the real issue. He obviously had noticed how antsy I was during the meeting.

"You may as well just lay it on the line," I said, sighing. "I can tell something's on your mind."

"Well, now that you mention it…" He crossed his massive arms over his equally massive chest. Like I said, I was big, but this dude was hard and cut like a mountain. "I noticed something was off during the meeting, Benny."

"Uh-oh, do I even want to know what you're thinking?"

My sponsor was sometimes *too* observant. And I hadn't yet decided if that was a blessing or a curse.

Pinning me with a don't-try-and-bullshit-me roll of the eyes, he said, "When some of the other guys were talking about struggling with destructive behaviors, you looked uneasy as fuck."

Shit. It was time to play dumb. "You think so? How do you mean?"

"You were sighing heavily and moving around in your seat, like you were dying to speak up." *Damn creaky chairs!* "Is there something that didn't get brought up that's still weighing on you?"

I slipped into full busted, defensive mode, as evidenced when I snapped, "I haven't fallen off the wagon, if that's what you mean."

"That's great, but that's not what I mean. There are other things that can be just as destructive, Benny."

I calmed down an iota. He was only trying to help.

"Yeah, yeah, I know," I conceded.

Aw, fuck, I know exactly what he means. And it has nothing to do with donuts.

"So..." He eyed me knowingly. "I'm assuming you're back to calling up women from your little black book?"

I raised a brow. "You mean my famous puck bunny directory?"

He nodded, and I went straight to my best tried and true avoidance tactics. "First off, Tettersaw, it's not a 'little black book.' It's not even black, it's red. And it's more of a pamphlet."

He rolled his eyes again. "Yeah, okay, whatever you say."

"Actually," I continued, still avoiding shit like a mofo, "it's technically a notebook. But whatever it is, let me assure you that it's not a 'problem.'"

Graham snorted. "It's a problem if you're calling the women in it."

"Okay, so what if I am?"

"How often are you doing that?" he asked somberly.

I thought about it and confessed, "Since I got back into town, maybe once or twice a week?"

"Once or twice a *week*!" Graham shook his head. "Man, you're worse than I ever was. And I was pretty bad at the height of my career."

I blew out a breath and just fucking leveled with him. "My puck bunny directory isn't what's messing with me, Graham. Not today."

He grew über serious. "What do you mean?"

I ran a hand down my face. "Ah, fuck. So here's the thing. I picked up some chick last night at a casino. She wasn't even *in* my stupid directory."

Graham saw where that could be a problem, and said quietly, "She wasn't?"

"Nope. And we ended up at her house. Where, of course, one thing led to another. Once it all started, it was like a blur of crazy sex. I lost myself in it."

"Benny..."

"I know, I know. It gets worse. When I woke up, I couldn't even remember her fucking name. I just wanted out of there, dude. I don't even know why I went home with her in the first place. I just guess there's comfort in bad habits."

Looking worried as hell, Graham said, "A blur of crazy sex, huh? You sure you were totally sober?"

"I'm sure. I told you alcohol wasn't the issue." I dragged my hand through my unruly hair, tugging at the wild ends.

"So what *exactly* about last night has you so worked up today?" Graham carefully asked.

Shit, I was about to try to explain something I didn't even have a handle on. But I knew it was for my own damn good. That's why Graham had asked.

"Fuck, dude," I began. "Picking the girl up is the problem. Not the girl herself"—I waved a hand—"but how it all made me feel. Not knowing her in the slightest and her not being from the puck bunny directory... It was all one hell of an endorphin rush."

"Let me get this straight." Graham peered over at me thoughtfully. "You're telling me you got *more* of a rush from picking up a stranger than from simply calling some girl in your directory?"

"Yeah," I sighed. "I did."

My directory—and I wasn't proud of this—was a compilation of puck bunnies and, for lack of a better word, hockey whores. They were the women I kept on speed dial. It was bad enough I couldn't bring myself to destroy the damn thing, as I knew it wasn't good for me, but I sure as hell didn't care to start up a whole new problem. Picking up strange women fell into that "whole new problem" category.

With that in mind, I conceded a little.

"I know what I did wasn't good for me. Shit like that is an escalation and could easily lead me back to the kinds of behaviors that almost destroyed my career."

"And nearly destroyed *you*, Benny," Graham reminded me.

"Yeah, right," I replied. Hey, at least I could admit it.

Graham poured himself a cup of coffee, and as he stirred in that shitty powder creamer crap, he said, "You need to ask yourself *why* you keep doing this sort of stuff. Why do you have problems dealing with women in healthy ways?"

I gave him a look and, feeling boxed-in, snapped, "Do I really need to explain the obvious, dude?"

"Look, okay, I know. The chase, the pursuit, those things are exciting for men. Hell, I've been there myself. But hooking up with random women, from your directory or otherwise, speaks of something deeper, some unmet need."

He was going all "sponsor" on me, and I half expected him to say my unmet need was that I didn't feel loved. Fuck that. Maybe it was true, but I'd never admit it. Hell, I was okay. I had a family that loved me back up in Canada. And I even had pets!

Okay, sure, my "pets" were fish in an aquarium. But they loved me in their own fishy kind of way.

I knew what Graham was really driving at, that I needed the love of a good woman to straighten my ass out. But before I'd admit *that* to him, I'd die.

In my most snarky tone, I stated, "Yeah, I'm pretty sure my *unmet need* is to blow my fucking load."

He shot me the finger.

I was being a dick. Graham was only trying to help. But my defenses were way the hell up. Fucking random women was not exactly stable behavior, I knew that. It'd never lead to anything meaningful. Plus, it was the kind of shit that had led to my other addictions, the ones that landed me in rehab in the first place.

I didn't want to go back to that place in my life, but... "Damn it, Graham, I have to have something."

He wasn't buying it and made me pledge to cut down on the ladies.

"Maybe give a girl you really like a chance?" he said.

"If only I could find one," I muttered.

"Put away the directory, Benny. And for the love of God, stay away from random pick-ups. Maybe then you might."

I wasn't sure about all that, but I promised to try.

I would, too.

At least I still had donuts.

3

BACK IN THE GAME OF LIFE

ELIZA

I expected the first months of adjusting to life with my parents, and being a parent myself, to be a challenge. But I actually took to it quite easily. Ava kept me busy, busy, busy, as did classes at UNLV once they started up.

I fell into a routine the minute the fall semester got underway. My life was going to school and taking care of baby, going to school and taking care of baby, going to school and taking care of baby…

You get the picture.

Who needed a life as a single young woman, anyway? Not me. I kind of liked hiding away.

Or did I…?

One warm September day—*ha, like there are any other kind in Las Vegas*—my mom pulled me aside. She was excited as could be that she just happened to have a spare ticket for a Wolves preseason game that night.

"It's for you," she said when I stared blankly at the piece of paper in her outstretched hand.

That's right, Eliza, there's still a whole world out there. Remember that crush you have on Benny Perry? Maybe it's time to work on making it happen, maybe move Benny from fantasyland to reality.

"You still like hockey, right?" my mom asked worriedly.

She needn't have been concerned. The old me was coming back. She'd been stymied, not destroyed. Since the day we left DC, I'd been rising to the surface, ready to return to a full life.

Here was my chance to start, to quit hiding. And more importantly—to see Benjamin freaking Perry in action!

"Of course I still like hockey," I replied. "I *love* hockey, Mom." *And I lust for a certain hot player*, I silently added.

"Good," she sighed. "I was so afraid *that guy*"—she waved the ticket around like she might be imagining smacking *that guy* with it—"had ruined hockey for you."

It didn't take a rocket scientist to figure out, even if she didn't know his identity, she hadn't forgotten Ava's father was a hockey player.

I rolled my eyes. I'd never let *him* win.

"Mom, that asshole could never make me hate hockey." I snatched the ticket from her hand. "In fact, I'd love to go to the game tonight."

She smiled brightly, giving me her best way-to-go-Eliza grin. "Good," she said.

It was decided. But then I panicked, remembering my new responsibilities.

"Wait, what am I thinking?" I shook my head and tried to hand the ticket back. "I can't go."

"Why not, Eliza?"

"What about Ava? There's only one ticket."

Would a baby even need one to get in? I could hold her, right?

I rethought that craziness quickly. Taking an infant to a rowdy arena where a stray puck could fly up into the crowd—*gasp!*—suddenly didn't sound like such a great idea.

That was it, I couldn't go.

Or could I?

Mom, apparently thinking on the same lines, offered to watch Ava.

I wavered, though. "I don't know."

"She'll be fine, Eliza," she assured me. "I babysit her all the time while you're at school."

"I know, I know. That's not the issue. I just don't want to take advantage."

Mom assured me, "You're not taking advantage, sweetheart. You'd be doing *me* a favor. I love spending time with my granddaughter. So go, have fun." She touched my shoulder lightly. "Maybe someone nice will be seated next to you."

Did she mean a guy? I rolled my eyes.

"Mom, I'm not going to the game to find a boyfriend."

Or was I? Benny would be there, right? And I sure liked him. What if I somehow ran into him? What if we hit it off?

Stop, Eliza. Dad would never let that happen.

"I know, honey." Mom replied. "I didn't mean a man. I was thinking maybe you'd meet a new friend."

"Because that's so easy to do," I murmured sarcastically, already jaded at twenty-one.

"Eliza, really…" Another Mom head-shake, and then, "You have to try a little here."

She was right. I wanted my life out here in Vegas to be about more than Ava and school. At least, I thought I did. Making friends could complicate things, though. I had a secret I had promised to keep…to *that guy.*

I hated that I'd agreed to Ava's father's restrictive terms. Keeping quiet about him had led to keeping secrets in general. Really, what was I even thinking? Better to stay on the sidelines of life. There was no reason to go to this game. There'd be no Benny Perry in my life. There'd be no new friends.

"I should just stay home," I murmured dejectedly.

"Oh, honey, please reconsider. You really need a night out."

It took some more convincing on her part, but I finally gave in. "Okay, okay, you're right. A night out might do me some good."

"That's the spirit, Eliza. So you'll go to the game?"

"Yes."

"And you'll be sure to have fun?"

"I'll try, Mom."

She was beaming by that point, but taking into account my dad's stance on me and hockey players I figured it was wise to ask, "Are you absolutely sure Dad's okay with this?"

"He's the one who got you the ticket, Eliza."

"Wow."

I was beyond surprised. If my overprotective father was putting aside his commitment to keep me away from his players, I really must be a mess.

He was waving the white flag, calling a truce, so I would, as well. I wouldn't push things. I'd simply watch and admire Benny Perry from up in the stands. I would *not* actively try to meet him. Again I told myself I'd go to the game and come straight home. No detours to the locker room area or anywhere where I might run into a player. I had access because of who my dad was, but I wouldn't use it. The temptation might be too much if I actually met Benny. I could want to touch him, maybe do other things to him, and with him.

No!

But I sure could look.

And look I did that night. Before the first puck was dropped, I searched the ice for number twenty-nine.

I found him over by the bench, taking off his helmet to adjust a strap or something.

God, even from afar, he was much more stunning in person. His shoulders and chest were crazy-wide. And his legs, those things were damn tree trunks.

I sighed. I had a major weakness for big guys. I loved how they could make me feel so much smaller than my five feet one inches of height, especially when I was *under* one.

A little shiver ran down my spine, and I was suddenly more into Benny than ever.

He wasn't just fun to look at, though. He was a great player and had real personality on the ice.

I liked how he took chances. And I loved that he taunted the opposing team's players mercilessly.

One guy got so fed up that he tried to punch Benny in the face.

"Oh, no," I gasped. "Don't you dare mess with that amazing bone structure."

That earned me a few curious glances…and a giggle from the girl next to me.

"He's a hottie, right?" I said to her.

Wow, I was really coming out of my shell. Mom would be proud.

The girl next to me agreed, "He is really cute."

She was about my age, and though stunning in the looks department, seemed really approachable. I was about to try and engage in more conversation with her, but my attention was drawn back to the ice when the wannabe-face-marring player stopped on his way to the penalty box and started yapping at Benny.

I could read Benny's lips as he said, "Anytime, fucker."

Designated "fucker" went at Benny again, but one of the linesmen grabbed him and ushered him away.

When the official's back was fully turned, Benny shot "fucker" the finger, along with a big grin.

I laughed, and so did my seat neighbor. I could've watched Benny all night, even when he wasn't on the ice. But the game itself was pretty exciting and fun. Something I was reminded of every time the girl next to me stood to holler or cheer.

I suddenly wanted Mom to be right—I wanted to become friends with this hockey-loving girl.

God, I was such a nerd.

Later on in the game, during the third period to be specific, the seeds of a friendship were finally sown when the right winger on Benny's line, some dude named Nolan Solvenson, scored a sweet goal that put the Wolves up by one.

That's when my seat neighbor went just about nuts.

"Oh my God," she squealed, turning to me excitedly. "I think we're definitely going to win this one."

I nodded and agreed, "I think so, too."

She held out her hand. "I'm Lainey, by the way."

She seemed so confident, and I could see why. She was a true beauty, what with her shiny mahogany hair and cool turquoise eyes.

"I'm Eliza," I replied, suddenly feeling a little awkward and shy.

My own confidence only went so far, so good thing Lainey had self-assurance for the both of us.

"I totally should've introduced myself earlier," she went on, totally at ease, "seeing as we've been sharing space all night."

"Aw, that's okay. The game's been really engrossing."

"It has," she agreed. And then she asked, "Are you here all alone?"

I didn't read anything into her question, but began to wonder what-the-heck when she burst into laughter.

"Oh, crap, what you must think," she said, blushing. "I swear I didn't mean that as a come-on. For real, I'm not trying to pick you up or anything."

I laughed. This was definitely a girl after my own heart. I needed to let her know there was no need to apologize, as I was far from uptight.

"I wouldn't have cared if you were," I replied, shrugging. "You're very pretty, so if I did swing that way, I'd definitely let you."

We both started laughing at that one, and our friendship was born.

"Still, let me explain," she went on. "What I was *trying* to ask was, since you're here all alone, is it because you know someone on the team...or are you just a totally rabid Wolves fan."

Hmm, which one is she?

"I'm not here for anyone," I replied. "And I don't know about the rabid part, but I'm definitely a Wolves fan." I paused. "I kind of *have* to be these days."

That piqued her interest. "Why's that?" she inquired.

"Coach Townsend is my dad."

"Oh, wow, no way. Coach T seems like a really nice guy. He's a great coach, that's for sure."

She peered over at the bench, and I followed her gaze. My dad was taking advantage of a time-out the other team had called and was barking out some last-minute instructions to his players.

They were listening intently, and I realized then that my dad really was an amazing man. He was worthy of my respect, even if he did drive me nuts on occasion.

"So they say," I murmured.

And then, I guess because I hadn't had anyone to talk to in what seemed like forever, I began over sharing.

"This is all kind of new to me," I blathered. "Watching a Wolves game, that is. Last season I missed most of them, except for the ones that were broadcast nationally."

Lainey looked utterly confused. "Were you living somewhere else?"

"I was."

I paused, wondering if I should go on. What if I said too much? That wouldn't be good.

I tried to wrap things up by simply stating, "I was away at college."

That didn't kill the subject like I hoped it would. Nope. Lainey's questions kept on coming. Not for any nefarious reason, the poor girl was just trying to make conversation.

"Oh, yeah, which school?" she asked.

I sighed. "Georgetown. You know, in DC."

She looked impressed, and I guess she was since she then said, "Wow, that's a really good school."

"Yeah, it is. I liked going there."

A feeling of wistfulness came over me, and I looked away.

Quietly, she said, "Did you graduate? Is that why you're back in Las Vegas?"

Oh, crap, I should steer away from this topic now.

But did I?

No.

I suddenly and inexplicably began sharing even more. Go figure. I rambled on about school…and where I was now…and finally wrapped it up with this stupid explanation for coming back: "I really missed the warm weather."

Oh, Eliza, what a lame excuse for changing schools.

I couldn't tell her anything more or too much would come out, so I switched the focus from me to her.

"Are you in school?" I asked.

She shook her head. "No. I graduated this past spring."

"Oh, yeah? From where?"

"University of Minnesota."

"Wow, that's a long way away. Did you find a job out here? Is that what brought you to our sunny little mecca?"

She rolled her eyes. "I wish. I did find *a* job recently, but it's nothing career-related."

"What kind of job is it?" I inquired, genuinely curious.

"I'm cocktail waitressing at one of the casinos."

"Ah."

She gave me a commiserating look, and I knew then that we were destined to become friends. We were too much alike. Neither one of us had this life thing figured out.

She shared with me then that she was living with her sister and her sister's fiancé.

"But that was never my plan" She sighed. "I was living with my parents for awhile when I was looking for a job back east. They were driving me crazy, though, so I had to get out of there."

"I know the feeling," I murmured. "Parents have a way of doing that."

We sighed in unison, then I asked, "So your sister and her fiancé…
Are they big hockey fans, too?"

Smiling like she had a secret and it was a good one—see, a girl after
my own heart—she said, "You could say that. It was my sister's fiancé
who got me the ticket for the game tonight."

"Well, it's a really good seat," I mused. "So your ticket procurer is
either a player…or someone high up in management."

"He's not in management," she slyly retorted.

"He's a player, then?"

The action picked up on the ice, and caught up in the game once
more, we tabled that discussion.

As we watched the players skate from one end of the ice to the
other, I remarked, "Wow, the game's really opening up."

"It sure is," Lainey agreed, her eyes glued to the ice.

Though the lines were changing fast, and players from both sides
were out for short shifts only, Lainey seemed zoned in on one player in
particular—Nolan Solvenson.

Maybe that's her sister's fiancé?

I was about to guess he was the ticket-giver, but then I recalled that
Nolan was supposedly unattached.

Oh, hell. Instead of speculating, I just flat-out asked, "So who's your
sister's fiancé? Is he out there on the ice right now?"

It seemed he was, as she pointed to the captain of the team,
centerman Brent Oliver.

"She's engaged to that guy right there," she stated proudly.

"No way."

The puck careened to Brent at that exact second, and as it landed
on his stick he flicked it into the other team's empty net, prompting me
to add, "I can't believe your sister's engaged to freaking Brent Oliver."

The whole time I'd been talking with Lainey there'd been something familiar about her. And I suddenly knew what it was.

"Wait a second." I turned to her. "I know who you are. I've seen you in pictures. You're Brent's fiancée Aubrey's little sister, right?"

"I am."

"I see the resemblance now," I continued. "It's uncanny, actually."

She laughed softly. "We hear that a lot."

The game came to an end—with a Wolves victory, yay!—and since I'd promised my mom I'd come straight home, I stood, set to leave.

I couldn't help but hesitate, though. I hated that the game was over and my time with Lainey was done for good.

But did it have to be?

No.

I wanted to stay in touch, so I said, "Hey, I really have to get going, but—"

A guy behind Lainey asked her a question then, and when she turned back to me I lost my nerve and decided to just wrap things up.

"It was really fun talking with you, Lainey." I started to turn away. "I'm sure I'll see you around."

She called out my name and I spun back around. "Yeah?"

"Hey, if you don't have anywhere you need to be, you're more than welcome to join me in the family lounge. I drove in with Brent and he's my ride home, so I have to wait for him in there. Otherwise, I'd suggest something else, something more fun. Still, we can make it fun. I'm sure Brent will be tied up for a while. The media will want to interview him about that goal at the end of the game."

"Yeah," I agreed. "I'm sure they will."

"So what do you think? Are you, Eliza Townsend, up for the challenge of drinking all the free coffee in the lounge?"

She looked fun and devious, like she had a bigger plan at hand.

Ugh, I wanted to say yes, but I couldn't.

"We'll be right next to the locker room," she added, sweetening the pot. "That means if we position ourselves *just right* by the door, there's a good chance a half-naked player will walk by and we'll see more than we should."

She winked, and oh, how I wanted to say I'd go. I mean, crap, Benny could be the half-naked player strolling by.

Tempting as it was, there was just no way. I had to get home to relieve my mom from babysitting duty. Plus, I really wanted to see Ava.

And then there was my dad…

Sighing, I said, "I'd really love to hang with you, Lainey. Seriously, I would. I mean, shit, who wouldn't be up for admiring hot hockey player butts, right?"

"We could even rate them," she interjected, brow raised.

"Tempting," I replied. And it was.

Scrunching up her face, she suddenly amended, "Maybe I won't rate Brent's ass, though. That would be too weird."

I laughed. She was funny, and I wanted to hang with her. I was even willing to take a chance with my dad. But I'd promised my mom, and I couldn't fuck her over.

"Another time?" I threw out.

"Sure."

We talked a few minutes more, and then I readied to take off. "Well, like I said, it was great meeting you."

"Yeah. You, too, Eliza."

I took out my phone. "Do you want to exchange numbers before I go? We could do something fun some other time. Player butt ogling, or anything, really."

Lainey smiled, and we exchanged info.

I left happy with how the night had turned out.

I'd have to thank my mom. Not only had I met a new friend, but, more than ever, I was feeling like my old self.

"Benny Perry, you better watch out," I murmured.

I wanted to meet him, and I was going to meet him.

Nothing could stop me now.

THAT'LL FIX COACH

BENNY

My head was in a better place once the season officially began. I was staying away from puck bunnies—well, for the most part—and not even eating *that* many donuts. Needless to say, I was proud of my progress.

I was also scoring like crazy. But I swear it was like Coach Townsend had it out for me. And that, my friends, was bullshit.

As long as you didn't count my womanizing—which, as established, I'd cut way the fuck back on—I hadn't done anything to deserve his wrath. Save for sneaking in a donut or two every few days. But with the way we worked out, a few extra calories shouldn't matter. I was where I was supposed to be weight-wise, anyway.

Well, more or less. I had gained one pound.

Maybe that was what had Coach T all up in my grill one morning after practice.

"Your concentration is off and your work ethic is for shit, Perry," he barked as he sidled up to me, like, real close. "You need to think about the stick in your hand a little more than the one in your pants," he hissed.

Oh, so it wasn't the extra pound that had him all wound up. He must've heard about a recent conquest of mine. How he always found out about this shit was beyond me. But singling me out, while other guys on the team did the exact same thing, was screwed up.

The more I thought about it, the angrier I got.

When Coach skated away, I made the mistake of smacking my stick on the ice and mumbling a very loud, "This shit is fucked up."

Coach T heard me, of course, and was back in my face in a heartbeat. "I hope you're happy, Perry," he yelled. "You just earned your smartass self *and* the rest of the team an extra half hour of drills this morning."

My teammates, some of who were already off the ice, grumbled as they turned around and skated back on. No one held it against me, though. After we finished with the extra drills and were convened back in the locker room, the usual ribbing commenced.

Dylan Culderway, a premier defenseman on our team, kicked things off by making a joke about how I better keep my horny self far away from Coach's daughter.

"I heard she's back in town," Dylan said.

"Oh, yeah," I mumbled disinterestedly, "where was she before?"

I didn't keep fucking tabs on these kinds of things.

"D.C., apparently," Dylan replied. "At college, I guess."

"Oh, really?" I perked up. So she was young, hmm... "You say she's back in Vegas?" I said.

"Yep."

I then asked a very pertinent question, "Is she hot?"

Dylan laughed. "Dude, Coach already has it out for you. I'm telling you, he'd annihilate your ass if you ever tapped his precious daughter."

Ignoring the warning, I replied, "What's her name?"

"Eliza."

"Eliza, eh?"

I liked the way it rolled off my tongue. Better yet, this could be my chance to exact revenge on Coach T for treating me like a pariah.

"What does this Eliza look like?" I asked Dylan. I didn't want to hit on the wrong girl.

"Not sure," he replied. "I've never met her. Since her dad doesn't want her around any hockey players, I don't think she's ever been here at the arena."

But then Jaxon Holland, a second-line center, jumped in and said, "I've met her."

"And…?" I queried.

He let out a low whistle. "She's a hot piece of ass, just your type, Perry. A tiny, little thing…" He outlined an hourglass shape with his hands, and I was salivating by the time he got to "…curvy as fuck, too."

"That's it. I have to meet this Eliza," I declared.

"Go for it." Holland laughed.

He could be a real dog like me, as demonstrated when he went on to say, "There's nothing better than drilling a chick with hips like that. You can really grab on and go to town."

When he mimicked a fucking motion, we all cracked up.

Except for Brent Oliver, captain of our team, who was frowning as he said, "You better stay away from Eliza, Benny. Dylan's right. Coach T is crazy protective of her. He despises the idea of his daughter dating a hockey player."

"Huh, I wonder why that is?" I mused.

Brent shrugged. "I don't know, but weren't you here the day he told us she was off-limits?"

I thought about it and couldn't recall. "I must've been running late that day," I concluded.

"Probably busy buying a chocolate donut," someone yelled.

I swung my head around to see who the smartass was. Probably one of the younger guys, as the rookies always had commentary.

"Who said that?" I wanted to know. No one fessed up, and I mumbled, "Pussies."

"Anyway," Brent resumed, "Coach T made a big point of telling us to stay the fuck away from her. He promised there'd be consequences if any of the players asked her out."

"Ha, ask her out? Who said I wanted to *date* her?" I volleyed back, mimicking, slow and easy, the same fucking motion Jaxon had a few minutes ago.

Everyone lost it then, including Brent. Though I did hear him mutter under his breath, "It's your funeral, man."

It'll be worth it, I thought.

I liked that Eliza was off-limits. What a stellar way to get back at Coach for riding me so hard and unnecessarily lately.

And shit, fate must've been on my side. Or it was like I was predestined to meet her or something. Why else would it happen that, not ten fucking minutes later, Nolan—who'd been in the showers and missed the whole Eliza discussion—asked if I'd like to join him, Lainey, *and* the coach's daughter for lunch that afternoon.

I almost lost it right there. But, playing it cool, I casually replied, "Sure, why not? I have nothing better to do."

Nolan breathed a sigh of relief, like he was counting on me saying yes.

Apparently he was, seeing as he blew out a breath and flat-out stated, "Thank fucking God. Now I won't be forced to listen to fashion and makeup talk the entire time I'm eating Cobb salad."

Nolan, who incidentally *loved* Cobb salad, was making it sound like the whole lunch date was an annoyance.

Shit, I knew better. It was all an act. Dude couldn't wait to see Lainey. That girl had my friend by the balls. And I suspected he secretly loved it.

I sometimes wondered what was *really* going on between them. Why they didn't just come out as a couple, I had no clue. It was like they were engaging in some kind of weird mating ritual.

Well, whatever. It wasn't my place to judge. I had my own mating ritual to work on—fucking Coach's daughter.

I got right to work on that an hour later when we met up with Eliza and Lainey at the restaurant. Shit, the boys had been right—Eliza Townsend was sexy as fuck. Better still, she knew a lot about hockey and was fun to be around.

Seducing her was going to be a piece of cake.

I flirted with her a bunch, and she was receptive as fuck. She was wearing this sexy sundress that was giving me a boner. The thing was cut real low and showcased her plump, juicy tits to perfection.

Every time she laughed over some silly thing I'd purposely said, they jiggled enticingly. I couldn't help but sneak in many peeks. And though I was subtle about it, she caught me a time or two.

Instead of glaring at me like she was offended, she smiled encouragingly.

Fuck, I was so in.

She kept right on smiling and giggling at my jokes, even the not-so-funny ones, all through lunch. I liked this chick, and it seemed she liked me. She was innocence and sin, my favorite combination.

There was something about her milky skin, big green eyes, and reddish-blonde hair. Girl was just rocking a super-sexy vibe, making me conclude that Coach's daughter was one of those girls who looked pure, but was anything but.

I wanted to put my sexing-her-up plan into action, and I wanted to do it right away. But to succeed in a way Coach would never suspect, I had to be clever. That's why when I asked her to the game that night, I was sure to include Lainey.

Nolan gave me a funny look, like he was wondering what I was up to. But he ended up agreeing it was a nice idea.

Nice, my ass.

I made sure Eliza knew the invitation was really all for her. That's why I gave her a sneaky wink.

"What do you think?" I asked her then. "You up for watching us play tonight?"

"I'd love to go," she replied, along with a sly wink of her own.

Fuck, this was so on.

Coach T wanted to ride my ass for no good reason? Well, I was about to give him something to really whine about.

I planned to do whatever it took to get sexy Eliza Townsend on my cock.

5

PUREED SWEET POTATO DELIGHT

ELIZA

At the lunch date Lainey set up so I could meet her sort-of boyfriend, Nolan, Benny came along.

Yay!

My spirits soared when I saw him walking into the restaurant with Nolan. I'd been angling to meet him, and here, finally, was my chance.

What a chance it turned out to be!

Benny was awesome. He was as adorable off the ice as he was on.

By the time our entrees had arrived, I decided I really liked him. I couldn't help it. Benny was witty and funny and charming as all get-out. He was so damn handsome, too. Way better up close than from far away. He and Nolan had worn suits, and Benny was rocking his to the nth degree.

His bangin' body made me want him so badly. His perfect face did, too. He had his dark blond mane slicked back, highlighting his amazing bone structure and eyes.

Oh, those eyes, a girl could get lost in them. They were *amazing*, a much deeper and richer shade of green than my own.

I just liked him, okay?

And I wanted him in all sorts of ways.

Benny seemed into me, too. I caught him ogling my boobs a number of times, and I totally didn't care. I wanted him to be as attracted to me as I was to him. That's why I was thrilled when he invited me—well, and Lainey—to the game that night.

Flying high and feeling more desirable than I had in a long time, I returned home to Ava. My mom informed me she'd been good, but was fussier than usual while I was out.

I went to her and let her nurse, even though she was pretty much weaned over to formula. Occasionally, though, at times like these, we both found it to be a comfort.

As I held Ava close to me, I told her all about my lunch with Benny, snickering when I got to the part about how I'd noticed him staring at my chest.

"He's clearly a boob man, Ava," I said. "I caught him sneaking a peek at least a half dozen times."

A completely uninterested Ava peered up at me, nursing away.

"He was gazing at these things almost as hungrily as you do sometimes," I went on.

I left out that it wasn't nourishment Benny was after. He wanted me. And that was a good thing since I was lusting after him harder than ever.

Still, I knew I'd have to take things slowly. No jumping into bed with a hot hockey player, not like the last time. Maybe some messing around, but no fucking.

"I have to think of you now," I declared.

Ava made a gurgle noise of assent.

Lightly touching my daughter's dark hair and marveling at how it had grown in so thickly—a deep, rich brown like her absentee father's—I softly added, "My former recklessness is how you got here. But, sweetie,"—I held onto her, my heart bursting with love—"I wouldn't change a thing."

Despite the fact that Ava made me feel a kind of love that was deeper and stronger than any I'd ever known, one baby was enough for now. Hell, people still didn't know I had a child, thanks to her jerky dad.

No one at school had any idea, and certainly no one who played for the Wolves knew anything. Not even Lainey was aware of Ava.

It was my own damn fault, and I didn't know how to fix it now. I'd allowed Ava's father to dictate my life when he wasn't even a part of it. I hated this hole I'd dug for myself. I'd never intended for it to go on so long, but I could see no easy way out. It'd gone on long enough that people were bound to be angry with me. And they had every right.

"What should I do?" I asked Ava. "I'm sure in a mess."

Of course she had no answer, so I decided to do nothing for now. I simply stowed away my concerns for another day.

At the game that night, I was decked out in full Wolves regalia. And I'd put my worries behind me. I was having way too much fun anyway, watching Benny play fantastic hockey.

He smiled up at me once, gave me a thumbs up even.

Damn, I couldn't believe my crush was attracted to me. How often does *that* dream come true?

Flying high, I leaned over to Lainey and gushed, "Benny is just *so* good at playing hockey."

"Nolan, too," she replied, a little dreamily herself. "They're both amazing players."

"Mmm-hmm," I concurred.

Nolan scored then on a highlight reel-worthy pass from Benny.

Lainey and I high-fived, and she said, "I love when we're right."

I laughed, noting, "For sure."

Cocking her head and peering over at me intently, she stated, "You know what?"

"What?"

"You and Benjamin Perry would make a really cute couple."

"You think so?" I replied, acting clueless.

"I don't *think so*, Eliza. I know so."

She went on to inform me that her new mission was going to be to hook us up. That sounded good to me, obviously.

I used that moment to get the goods on Benny, and Lainey had fantastic news—there was no girlfriend in his life.

"There hasn't been one for ages," she informed me.

"Great," I replied.

But then there was some bad news, as well. "Benny has a reputation for being a bit of a player. So be careful, Eliza."

Crap.

"I will," I assured her.

I reminded myself—and her—of something I believed to be true. "Bad boys fall in love, too, you know?"

"Yes, they do," she softly agreed, though I was pretty sure she was thinking of Nolan on that one.

When the game ended, Lainey sent a text to Nolan, asking if he and Benny were up for a late-night dinner with us.

"I'm sure they'll say yes," she said confidently as she hit *Send*.

But dinner was a no-go, to both our dismay.

"Shit, that sucks," I said.

Lainey sent another text to Nolan, this time fishing for a reason why they couldn't go.

He was really evasive in his reply, and that made me suspect— rightly so—that their mystery destination might be a strip club that had recently opened.

"I heard about it from my dad," I informed Lainey. "He was bitching about how it was just down the road from the arena and that could be a problem."

Lainey quickly came up with a plan to crash what had to be the boys' destination. Since it involved potentially spending time with Benny, albeit not in the most conducive atmosphere for getting to know one another, I was in.

Things didn't go quite as planned, though. I ended up not seeing Benny at all, even though he was at the club and in the audience. Problem was Lainey and I only made it to the back of the joint. Where my crazy friend got roped into *dancing*—like, on a pole, on the stage, in front of all the guys.

That's a whole other story.

Anyway, I wasn't brave enough to get in on the dancing thing, so I waited backstage. At least I did until a grumpy bouncer booted me out. I had no choice then but to leave.

As I drove home, I felt sad that my opportunity to spend more time with Benny hadn't worked out.

Ah, but fate was on my side.

A week after the game and the fateful strip club outing, I ran into Benny, at, of all places, a local supermarket.

"Oh, sorry, miss," he mumbled distractedly when he rounded the corner and almost crashed his cart into mine.

He was peering down at his phone, the cause for his distraction and near-collision, and didn't realize it was me he'd nearly careened into.

"Hey, Benny," I said nonchalantly.

His head shot up. "Shit, Eliza. What are you doing here?"

"Just getting in a little shopping," I replied.

"Yeah, me, too," he said.

We were both a little nervous, which made me chuckle. We could be goobers together.

Curious as to what Benny was buying, I glanced in his cart.

Huh, it's loaded with lots of healthy stuff, like fresh fruits and vegetables.

No surprise there. But what did surprise me was the box of donuts buried under a pack of boneless, skinless chicken breasts.

I didn't want to bust him on his sneaky indulgence, as we all knew I had bigger secrets of my own. So, to be safe, I focused on the chicken, blurting out without thinking, "Wow, those breasts look really good."

That comment brought his attention to my own prominently displayed boobage. I was rocking a bright yellow tee that was tight as hell.

Benny, eyeing me up unabashedly, murmured, "Yeah, they sure do."

"Definitely a breast man," I whispered under my breath.

"What was that, Eliza? I didn't hear you."

He wasn't supposed to, so I waved him off. "Oh, it was nothing."

I should've kept the focus on my boobs. Maybe squeezed them together, or jumped up and down. Anything to keep him from turning his attention to what I happened to have in *my* cart.

Too late.

Like we were in some slo-mo video, his eyes drifted to the contents of my cart. I peered down at the same time, to see what he was seeing, and shit, it wasn't good. There were several jars of pureed baby food piled high, my Gerber selections in full and prominent view.

Crap, Ava had recently started on pureed baby food and freakin' loved the sweet potato ones. There were at least a dozen of those alone.

You better think fast, Eliza.

"What's with all the baby food?"

Benny's eyes drifted up to me, narrowing in suspicion.

"Do you mean that stuff in the jars?"

"Yes. That *stuff* in the jars, Eliza. It's baby food, right?"

"Indeed it is." I giggled nervously, swishing my hand around, buying time, as I scrambled for a believable explanation.

I finally came up with one, though it was a stretch.

"Believe it or not," I began, very serious-like, "the baby food is for me."

He looked confused. "For you?"

"Yes, for me. Mmm, mmm, good." I rubbed my tummy. *God, kill me now, I just can't stop.* "Baby food just happens to be an integral part of a new diet I'm trying. I just love the creamy taste."

I thanked God in that moment that I hadn't reached the diaper aisle. How would I have ever explained having diapers in my cart?

Brow furrowed, he said, "Really? I've never heard of any diet like that. Is there a name for it?"

"Why, it's the baby food diet, Benny."

"Huh, interesting. I hear about a lot of crazy diets from the guys, but I've never once heard of any baby food ones."

"You're kidding." I feigned shock. "You haven't? This one is, like, all the rage."

He shook his head. "Nope, haven't heard of it."

Laughing nervously, I kept digging that hole. You know the one, the one full of secrets and lies, the one that kept getting bigger and bigger.

"It's pretty new," I said. "That's probably why."

Still wary, he said, "Yeah, I guess."

I should've come clean then, but I was too caught up to stop.

"It's a really great plan," I blathered on. "Works wonders, I swear."

"I can see that," he said appreciatively as his gaze traveled up my body.

Well, this was a positive turn.

I was wearing bummy old jeans and that tight yellow tee. Nothing fancy, but with the way Benny was staring at me I felt like a star.

I moved right up to *super*star status when he went on to say, "Really, Eliza, you don't need to be on any diet. You look amazing just as you are."

I swooned at that. "Wow, thanks."

"So," he continued, back on his game as he crossed his big beefy arms, covered in tats, over his massive chest. "Does this baby food diet mean you've sworn off all adult food?"

I laughed nervously. "No, of course not."

"That's good to hear"—warm green eyes met mine—"because I was wondering if you'd like to go to dinner with me sometime."

Would I ever!

Play it cool, play it cool. I urged my exuberant self to chill.

Reveling in the power shift, I glanced at my nails, like they were suddenly infinitely interesting.

"Hmm, possibly," I murmured. "When were you thinking?"

Eagerly, he replied, "Any night that works for you would be fine with me. As long as we don't have a game, of course."

"What's the game schedule look like this week?" I inquired.

He uncrossed his arms and ran his fingers through his dark blond mane.

"Let's see, we have home games the next couple of days, but the weekend is free."

I pondered, then said, "My weekend is free, too." *Well, if my mom can babysit Ava.* "I think that might work."

Benny looked excited. "Great, I know just where we can go."

"Where's that?"

"There's an outstanding pasta place I like to frequent. It's quiet and real private. And the food there is out of this world, Eliza. I think you'd really like it."

"That sounds amazing," I said, dropping the play-it-cool act.

"Perfect. But I should warn you ahead of time…"

"Uh-oh, what now?"

He eyed up the baby food in my cart, but there was a sparkle of mischief in his eyes this time.

Smiling, he said, "I don't know if my little pasta place serves anything comparable to those, uh…" He coughed. "…delightful selections you have in there."

Sarcasm, I loved it. Benny was my kind of dry humor guy.

I was about to reply with something equally playful, but just then he leaned in for a better look inside my cart.

Jumping back, he just about gagged. "Ugh. What is that gross, orange-y brown crap in the jars on top? You have a fucking ton of those."

"Um…" *Ava's dreaded sweet potatoes, oh, no.*

He reached in and picked up a jar, going on to read the label out loud.

"Pureed sweet potatoes." Looking up, he raised a brow. "You do know what this stuff looks like, eh?"

"I never really thought about it," I honestly replied.

"I hate to say it," he began, "but it looks exactly like someone had a bad bowel movement and put it in a jar."

"Benny, that's disgusting," I exclaimed, though he was totally correct.

I kept thinking how he should see the stuff once it actually becomes a bad bowel movement. I wisely kept that one to myself.

It was taking all I had to not lose it right there, especially when Benny insisted, "Sorry, but it does, Eliza."

He was going to pay for this. I was about to have a little fun, as well.

Putting my hand over my heart, I feigned like I was hurt by his commentary.

"I can't believe you think that. The sweet potatoes"—I peered down at the jars as lovingly as I could for effect—"are the absolute best. You should try them sometime. Maybe you'll find they're fabulous, like I have."

The sweet potatoes were absolutely *not* fabulous. I'd snuck in a bite once while feeding Ava and gagged for over five minutes. But she sure loved them, so go figure.

Benny placed the jar back in the cart like it was burning his hand. "Uh, I think I'll pass," he muttered. "You can have them."

"Your loss," I stated.

We stopped then, looked at each other, and started to laugh.

"So about that dinner…?"

"Yes?"

"Are we on for the weekend? Say, Friday night?"

"Sounds good to me."

We made plans, agreeing not to tell anyone about our impending date. After all, my dad might castrate Benny if he ever found out he'd asked me out to dinner.

Yikes, we couldn't have that, could we?

Hell no!

Not before I had the chance to find out what kind of stick Benny was playing with.

And I didn't mean the one he used for hockey.

6

ELIZA TATTOOS MY HEART

BENNY

My date with Eliza was set, but I didn't tell anyone about it. Not even Nolan or Brent, my usual co-conspirators. I was waiting for the right time to leak the info, like after I'd nailed Miss Townsend. Yeah, sticking it *in* Coach's daughter was sure to stick it *to* Coach himself.

There was only one problem.

My devious plan to get back at Coach T wasn't holding the same appeal it first had. I genuinely liked Eliza. Like, above and beyond the initial crazy attraction I felt for her.

Eliza was pretty and sexy, but she was also sweet…and easygoing… and kind of really cool. There was nothing I didn't like about her, save for her taste for that repulsive baby food sweet potato slop.

Remembering our exchange at the grocery store made me smile. I liked how Eliza treated me like an ordinary person, not a hockey star. I always imagined myself ending up with someone like that. I'd never pursue a girl who wanted me for money or fame.

Eliza was nothing like that, thank Christ. She was honest and upfront about everything. Hell, she'd even confessed that she was on that weird baby food plan. That right there was some major trust.

A part of me wanted to give her a real chance. But then I felt scared, like, *shit, I like her for fucking real.*

I tried to fight it, but the part of me that genuinely liked her started to slowly push away the part that wanted to simply stick it to her.

Damn. Eliza had gotten to me more than I'd anticipated.

But was that such a bad thing?

I felt good, really good, when I thought about her. She made me excited about life, so much so that I actually took my puck bunny directory, the infamous red one I kept handy on the nightstand next to my bed, and threw it in the trash.

"There," I declared. "Now I can give Eliza a real chance, with no distractions."

Graham would be so proud I was taking his advice.

Then, I panicked. "Wait. Fuck Graham. And hold up on Eliza. I can't let a girl get under my skin like this."

I swiftly retrieved my puck bunny directory from the trash. But I made a concession—instead of leaving it conveniently located on my nightstand, I tossed it in a drawer.

A little progress in the right direction is better than none, right?

Over the next few days, I convinced myself the *only* reason why I'd put away my PB directory was because I needed to stay away from sex if I planned to keep a clear head about nailing Coach's daughter.

That soothed my troubled mind, but it made me feel all kinds of shady.

At least, it did until I learned something that made me feel not so bad. It seemed Eliza had a secret of her own. Why else would she be so damn adamant about me not picking her up at her house for our dinner date?

"I'll just meet you at the restaurant," she insisted when I called to confirm we were still on.

I'd received a text from Dylan after I'd vaguely asked him if he knew if Coach had plans to review game footage down at his office at the arena. He often did, and Dylan skated there on our days off. That's when the place was pretty much empty, so he'd know if Coach was there.

He texted back, *yeah, he's here. Looks like he will be for awhile, too.*

I shared my intel with Eliza and added, "Your dad will be there for hours. I can pick you up *and* drop you off. He'll never know we were out together."

"Mmm," she replied, "I still think it's better if we just meet out."

Why's she so damn insistent on this?

I was really wondering, but instead of pressing the issue, I relented. "Okay, we'll just meet at the restaurant."

After we disconnected, I remained truly mystified as to why I had to stay away from her house. I'd have understood if her dad was home. But he wasn't. He was at the arena and would be for hours.

"Maybe her mom's home and Eliza's worried she'll tell Coach I picked her up?"

Yeah, that had to be it.

My curiosity was sated, and I felt a hundred times better. Eliza wasn't so shady, after all. I was the one with a sneaky agenda, seeing as I was still planning to nail her. Maybe even tonight, if I was lucky.

When I arrived at the restaurant just as Eliza was getting out of her car, a few spaces away, I prayed it would indeed be tonight.

The girl was smokin'.

I jumped out of my car for a better view. *And, wow.* Eliza was sex personified. She was wearing her strawberry-blonde hair down and pulled forward over one creamy shoulder, all come-hither like. The sheath dress she had on fit her curves like a glove.

I was so engrossed in watching her saunter over to me that I barely noticed that she'd reached me and started talking.

"Hello, Benny, Earth to Benny." She waved her hand in front of my face. But still, I stood there, mouth open like a damn caveman—and as unresponsive as one.

Eliza's beautiful brows crinkled in concern. "Benny, you're worrying me. Did you get hit in the head with a puck at practice yesterday?"

Nope, more like I've been hit in the heart...right now...by you.

I wanted to say that, but it seemed a bit much for date numero uno.

I went instead with a safe and simple, "You look fucking amazing, Eliza. Maybe that's why I'm a little dazzled."

"Dazzled? Aww..."—*is she blushing?*—"thank you."

She was blushing, the cutest shade of pink. I didn't feel so bad that I'd turned into a blathering fool. Neither of us cared, as we stood there in the parking lot grinning at each other like two teenyboppers on a first date.

I knew then that this girl was going to be more than a conquest.

Gesturing to the door, I cleared my throat. "We should go in, eh?"

"Yeah, we should."

As we started in, I said, "So, Eliza, are you ready to experience the best pasta in the world?"

Her brows shot up. "That's quite a bold statement, Benny. But yes,

I think I am."

"Good. And always keep in mind that I'm a bold kind of guy."

I brazenly took her hand, and she murmured, "I see that."

Stick with me and I'll show you more, I wanted to say.

But the hostess then greeted us, with a lot of enthusiasm, I noted. She began to lead us back to a private table in a quiet room at the rear of the restaurant.

"This is perfect," Eliza leaned over and whispered. "We're the only ones in this back section."

"It's nice it worked out this way," I agreed.

I didn't share with Eliza that I'd called ahead and procured a private room for the evening.

The hostess suddenly stopped, telling us she had just realized she'd grabbed only one menu instead of two.

"I'm so sorry, Mr. Perry," she went on. "I'll be back in a minute with a second menu."

We were left standing there, and Eliza bumped my leg with her hip. She couldn't reach any higher. How cute was that?

Standing up on her tiptoes, she whispered in my ear, "I think our hostess is a little flustered by you."

"I don't know about that, Eliza."

"What? The girl couldn't even count out the correct number of menus. She's flustered, for sure."

"Nah," I replied. "She's probably just forgetful."

Another bump from Eliza, this one a little more forceful, and then, "Look at you, Benny, such a humble guy."

"Ha, hardly."

When she geared up to bump me again, I stepped behind her and caught her hips with my hands. She let out a little gasp when I gave a light squeeze.

"Mmm, Mr. Perry..." She leaned back against my chest, a little breathless. "Are you flirting with me?"

"I don't know, Miss Townsend. I think *you're* the one flirting with *me*."

Arching her sweet, rounded ass till it was damn near pressed in my groin, she breathed out, "You're right. I am."

She definitely was, and I rasped, "Hell, yeah."

Fuck, I wanted this girl in my bed. And with the way she kept leaning back into me, even as I grew rock-hard, I suspected she wanted the same thing.

Spinning around, she faced me.

Damn, I was done for right there.

"Benjamin," she said.

"Eliza," I replied.

I leaned down to kiss her, not even caring where we were. This girl was tattooing my heart, leaving her mark. And the ink was fucking spreading.

Wait, what?

My playboy side went nuts, but I made him shut the hell up. That's right, I was about to pursue something more than just sex with Eliza. Don't get me wrong. I still wanted her in my bed, now more than ever. But I no longer wanted to just fuck her to fuck over her dad.

I wanted her for her.

My lips grazed hers, and I drew in a sharp breath. She was vanilla and sugar and—

Someone cleared their throat.

"Uh, sorry to interrupt, but I have that other menu now."

The hostess was back. Talk about sucky timing.

With the moment ruined, Eliza and I broke apart.

I discreetly adjusted myself and, amid jumbled apologies, the hostess then seated us. She handed over the menus rapidly, before taking off.

"Finally," I murmured. "It's back to just us."

Oh, but I was wrong. The parade of restaurant employees had only just begun.

A kid came in next to pour us some waters.

And then a waiter appeared, to see if we wanted to start with drinks.

I, obviously, replied a big, fat *no* to that one.

It didn't mean Eliza had to abstain, so I looked over at her and asked, "Would you like something a little stronger than water to drink?"

"No." She shook her head. "Water's fine."

The waiter nodded and left.

I raised my glass of H2O and toasted, "Here's to us being alone again."

"Yes, but for how long?" She laughed and touched her glass to mine. "The employees here sure are über attentive," she noted. "But they keep popping in at the most inopportune times."

"You're not kidding," I agreed.

And then, in a more serious tone, I said, "So, Eliza,"—my gaze met hers—"what happened in here right before the hostess returned—?"

"Yes?"

"We should talk about it, eh?"

"Okay."

I blew out a breath, then laid it on the line. "Did that kiss feel as right to you as it did to me?"

She whispered, "It did."

I reached over and placed my hand over hers. This time there were no employee interruptions.

"I think we should talk about some other things, as well, Eliza."

I felt her tense up. *Odd.*

"Like what kinds of things?" she asked, nervous-sounding.

"Uh, nothing bad," I assured her. "I just think we better discuss some ground rules for dealing with Coach—er, I mean your dad."

Breathing a sigh of relief, which made me wonder what could possibly be worse than her overprotective father finding out about us, she said, "Oh, him."

"Yes, him."

The waiter returned to take our orders, and as Eliza was telling him what she wanted for dinner, my mind went somewhere else. I just couldn't wrap my head around the fact she didn't seem nearly as concerned about her father as I was.

How could that be?

And if that were the case, why had it been so important for me to stay away from her house? Why couldn't I have just picked her up? Even if her mom had been home and told her dad, what would it matter?

With our food orders in and Eliza looking over at me like she was wondering where I'd just gone, I cleared my throat and just straight-up asked, "Would your dad *really* flip if he knew we were going out?"

Instead of answering my question, she demurely queried, "Wait. Are you saying what I think you are, Benny?"

Oh, fun Eliza was back. Deflecting Eliza, yes, but fun Eliza, too.

"What do *you* think I'm saying?" I replied, playing along since I liked seeing her smile.

"That this is an official date?"

Hell, she knew it was.

I was all in on this flirting game, though, so gesturing to my finely tailored dark gray suit, I replied, "I sure hope this is a date. Otherwise, I'd have worn something more comfy. Like shorts and flip-flops."

"Ha." She glanced around at the classy interior. "You never would've been let in a place like this dressed like that."

Ah, but there's where she was wrong. The proprietors of this establishment—or any in this city, really—would never turn me away, no matter how sloppily I was attired. Just another perk of being a successful athlete.

Not wanting to dispel her illusion, nor sound like a cocky ass, I played along.

"Yeah, you're probably right. But"—my eyes met hers—"I assure you I wore this for you, not for any silly restaurant owners."

She smiled. "Then I guess that makes it official—this is definitely a date."

"Finally!" I leaned back and relaxed. "So now that that's established, what about your dad?"

She sighed. "I have to be honest, Benny. He wouldn't want us going out on any dates. Not to dinner, and, really, not anywhere."

"Why is that?" I was curious as hell as to why Coach was so protective of her.

"He just hates the idea of me with *any* hockey player," she replied, kind of evasive-like.

"Hmm, is there a story there that I should know about?" I inquired.

She was taking a sip of water and almost choked.

Once she recovered, she insisted, "No, there's no story. It's just the way he feels since he knows how players can be."

That one shut me up. I didn't want to go *there*. Still, it seemed a little too simple of an explanation. There *had* to be more to her dad not wanting her to date hockey players.

This was a date, though, and I wanted Eliza to have a good time, not feel all stressed out.

Leaning back, I crossed my arms and returned to the topic of Coach and me, instead of *why* he didn't want Eliza going out with hockey players.

"I guess I'm really taking a chance here, then," I remarked, chuckling.

"Why do you say that?"

"Well, if your dad finds out about tonight, he could retaliate."

"How do you mean?"

I thought about it. "He could encourage ownership to put me on the trading block."

She rolled her eyes. "No way would that ever happen. You're part of his top line, Benny. He may be overprotective about me, but he's not crazy."

"You have a point there," I conceded, feeling a little less worried.

Our dinners arrived then, and that discussion came to a merciful end. Besides, I was too busy devouring the best ziti known to mankind to talk…or worry…or whatever.

Eliza seemed just as into her carbonara dish.

"Is it good?" I asked when I came up for air.

"It's amazing, Benny."

I nodded approvingly. "Best pasta ever, eh?"

"It may very well be."

I was happy Eliza was happy, and that probably meant something. *Yeah, like you really like her a lot, idiot.*

"True," I murmured.

"What was that?" she asked. "I couldn't hear you."

"Oh, nothing," I replied.

Dinner ended as fast as it had begun. The waiter cleared our plates and dropped off a dessert menu. I picked it up before Eliza got to it and noticed immediately there was something on it I just *knew* Eliza would love.

"Would it be okay if I ordered our desserts?" I asked as I hid the menu by turning it over.

Eliza looked uncertain. "Um, yeah, sure, I guess. Can I have a hint of what you have in mind, though?"

She seemed worried I'd pick something terrible, but this was in the bag.

"I'd prefer it'd be a surprise, if that's okay?"

"What are you up to, Benny?" she asked, smiling.

I smiled right the hell back and told her, "You'll see. You're going to love this."

"Would we be able to split whatever it is," she asked then. "I'm really stuffed from dinner."

Whoa, that right there kind of threw me. I wasn't sure I'd like what I planned to order for Eliza.

Eh, what the hell.

When the waiter returned, I discreetly pointed to the third item down on the list of selections.

He left, but forgot the menu, and Eliza, losing patience, snatched it up.

"Hey," I protested.

"Nope, no way am I not checking." She scanned down the menu. "I have to know what I'm about to eat. I mean, for all I know, it could be chocolate-covered crickets."

She was so endearingly weird. "There are no chocolate covered crickets on the menu, Eliza," I assured her.

"Hmm, I see that," she said, not looking up. "So which dessert *did* you order for us?"

I was feeling smug as I declared, "Check out that third one down. It's the one I ordered. Perfect, eh?"

Instead of expressing elation, as I fully expected, she mumbled a blah-sounding, "Oh."

Maybe she was looking at the wrong dessert? Why else would she look so…grossed out?

Shit, maybe they do have chocolate-covered crickets on the menu? I could've missed them. From the look on Eliza's face, it seemed a real possibility.

Worried my surprise was about to blow up in my face, I hastily declared, "I ordered the sweet potato tart. You love sweet potatoes, right?"

She'd said as much in the grocery store, and if she liked that runny crap in the jars she was sure to love it in tart form. Tarts had sugar, lots of sugar, so it had to be good, right? It was the sole reason why I, the sweet potato hater, was willing to give it a go.

But that look on her face…

"Did I get it wrong?" I humbly asked.

"No, no." She tried to force a smile. "I'm sure the sweet potato tart will be amazing."

"I sure hope it is," I murmured.

I was beginning to think chocolate-covered crickets might not have been so bad.

Dessert arrived, and Eliza and I hacked off bits of the tart at the same time. I raised my fork and said, "Here's to nothing."

Five seconds later, though, I was mumbling from around a

surprisingly delectable mouthful of goodness, "Damn, this is really good."

Eliza laughed and agreed, "It is delicious. You chose well, Benny."

I preened. "And here I was, thinking that jarred baby food slop was disgusting. Based on this tart—"

"No, no, wait." Eliza waved her fork in the air. "Trust me when I tell you that the jarred sweet potatoes are nothing like this. I definitely don't recommend them."

Huh?

Confused, I queried, "I thought you loved sweet potato baby food? That's what you said in the store."

She froze, then composed herself quickly.

"Oh, yeah, you're right. I do love those. I just meant the others aren't good. Like the peas and carrots and stuff."

"Okay, Eliza."

She was an enigma—contradictory at times, straightforward at others. But damn if I didn't like her all the more for it.

That was it. I wanted to see her again, as soon as possible. So I asked, "Do you like to go dancing?"

I had no idea why I threw that one out. I wasn't even into dancing all that much. It just sounded like something fun to do, and I thought Eliza might be into it.

Smiling, she peered over at me, amused. "Is that your roundabout way of asking me out on another date?"

"Maybe," I conceded.

"But this one's not even finished," she replied while licking her fork in a way that made my pants feel suddenly tight. "What if it all goes to hell, Benny?"

I leaned forward. "I guess it could, Eliza, but I'm willing to bet it won't. Let's be crazy and take a chance. Let's plan our next date. Is that forward enough for you?"

"Yes," she replied. "And I like the dancing idea. It sounds like fun."

"Good, then we're set."

"Honestly, Benny," Eliza sighed. "Tonight's been amazing. And I don't *really* expect things to go awry. But, at this point, even if they do, I'd still go out with you again."

I cocked a brow. "You'd give me a do-over, eh? That's nice to hear."

Suddenly no longer teasing, she said softly, "Do-overs are a must, Benny. And that goes for *everyone*."

Huh, interesting. It was like she was referring more to herself than to me. Nah, that couldn't be right.

I whisked that thought away and returned to concentrating on our date. It couldn't be over yet.

With dessert cleared and the bill paid, I asked Eliza, "What next, m'lady?"

She put her hand over mine and said, "I don't care. I'm up for anything. I just don't feel like going home yet. Do you?"

"No, not at all. You have anything in mind?"

She smiled coyly. "Hmm, actually I do. It might sound kind of crazy, though."

I assured her, "Crazy is right up my alley, girl."

"Okay, good. Then here's my idea… Let's go night swimming."

What? Huh? She did know we were in a desert, right?

"Night swimming," I murmured.

"Yes. What do you think?"

"I think it's a lot easier said than done, seeing as where we are."

I racked my brain to come up with a place to *swim* at *night* in the freaking *desert*.

I had nothing, but she pressed, "Oh, come on. You must know of *some* place we could go swim."

"I do," I said, "but it's not any place around here. If we were back in my hometown, I could find us a dozen fantastic lakes and ponds. But here, it's more of a challenge."

"Your hometown is where again?" she asked.

"Surrey, BC."

"Oh," she sighed. "I can see where that'd be a bit of a drive."

"Yep, it sure would be."

"Well…" She blew out a breath. "At this point, any place with water would work."

I cocked a brow. "You do know we're in a very vast desert, yes?"

She laughed. "True. But there are pools everywhere."

"Good point. In fact, there just happens to be a pool in my backyard."

"There is, is there?"

"A heated one, too."

"Ooh, no shrinkage."

"Eliza!"

A girl who could shock me was rare, but this one could.

A sly smile played on her lips, and it held a dozen dirty promises. Little Eliza had a naughty side, and I fucking loved it.

"Only thing is," I warned, "my house is a little ways from here."

She shrugged. "No problem. I can just follow you there."

"That works for me."

I laced our hands together and squeezed. We both knew there'd be more than night swimming happening tonight.

My house was on the outskirts of Vegas, pretty much all by itself, save for a few neighbors and a mall that had recently been built. Even so, that was a mile away.

So basically it was all desert, baby.

I liked the privacy, and I really liked the seclusion. But never more had I appreciated those things than when Eliza hopped out of her car and informed me her idea of night swimming had only one major rule—everyone had to take off their clothes.

"Damn, skinny-dipping?" I said.

"Yep," she confirmed.

I couldn't get us back to the pool fast enough.

I DON'T WANT TO BE ANOTHER NOTCH ON BENNY'S BELT

ELIZA

I liked Benny. I liked him a lot. He was wild and fun, and I needed that in my life. That's why I'd come up with the whole night-swimming-after-dinner idea. Plus, I really wanted to see Benny naked, hence the skinny-dipping stipulation.

Once we were back at his pool, I was thrilled I'd called for that no-clothes clause. Benjamin Perry naked was quite a sight to behold. He was just so big *everywhere*.

His shoulders were wider than I'd realized, and his broad, muscular chest was nothing short of spectacular, what with all the tats, intricate and beautiful every single one.

I moved down to his legs, thick with hard muscle. But what caught my eye was what he was packing *between* his legs. The length and the girth of him matched the rest of the man, making certain parts of me tingle in a way they hadn't in ages.

"Eliza, are you stalling?" Benny tilted his head, eyeing me suspiciously, because I was still fully clothed.

It was just that seeing how perfect Benny's body was, I'd developed a case of cold feet.

I mean, come on! How he could stand there so casually, with his arms crossed *and* completely naked, yet not one bit self-conscious was astounding. I guess all that nudity in the locker room made him immune to modesty.

Damn it, I can do this, I told myself. It'd been my idea, after all.

"I'm not stalling," I said as I was, uh, stalling.

Brow quirked, Benny mused, "Hmm, maybe I have this all wrong."

"Have what wrong?" I asked.

"Last I heard, skinny-dipping meant *all* a person's clothes had to go." He paused, reflected. "But I don't know. Maybe the rules have changed."

"No, the rules haven't changed," I replied.

His tone softened. "So why aren't you naked, babe?"

Why was I hesitating? If Lainey could take off her clothes in a seedy strip club, then surely I could do so in front of one man. Benny was a man I liked, after all.

But that was the problem.

I felt self-conscious about showing him my body. I'd lost most of the baby weight, so that wasn't my concern. Plus—bonus!—my boobs had remained kind of huge. It was just that I knew Benny had seen many women with great and fit bodies. I feared mine would pale in comparison.

He stepped toward me. "Eliza, if you've changed your mind that's fine. I can run over to the poolhouse"—he gestured to a brick structure, big as a small house, at the back of the pool—"and grab some swim trunks. There are ladies' swimsuits in there, too. I keep those around for parties. Would swimming in a suit make you feel more comfortable?"

No, no way. I could do this.

"I'm good," I said, not about to let societal pressures and my own insecurities screw up this night.

I reached around and unzipped my dress. Benny watched, hunger igniting in his smoldering gaze as I peeled down the top part. Since I'd not worn a bra, my boobs jiggled free.

"Fuck, Eliza," he groaned.

Benny was hard instantly. Not that I was focusing on that part of him or anything. Just damn, the thing was difficult to miss.

My dress fell to my feet, and, stepping forward in just a thong and heels, I narrowed the gap between us.

Benny rasped, "The shoes and thong have to go, too, babe."

I wasn't stalling now; I was simply enjoying the tease. To hell with all my taking-it-slow proclamations, wild Eliza was back.

Turning away, I giggled and jumped in the water. Benny was soaked in the resulting splash.

"Hey, no fair," he called out after me. "You little vixen, you still have on those shoes and—"

"No, I don't," I interjected as I reached down into the water and pulled off one heel, then the other.

"There." I threw my pumps up on the side of the pool. "Everything's off now."

"No, it's not, you cheater. Your thong's still on."

"So I see, Benny." I shot him an inviting smile. "Maybe you need to come in and *make* me take it off."

Oh, I was in for it now. And I totally didn't care.

Benny jumped in the water so quickly that all I caught was a blur of massive man. He was coming after me, like I wanted him to. Even so, I let out a little squeak as I swam away.

Laughing my ass off—this was the most reckless fun I'd had in a while—I made my way to the deep water.

"You wait till I get a hold of you, Eliza," I heard Benny bellow as he closed in on me.

"Too late, Benny," I called back over my shoulder as I reached the side of the pool and started sliding the thong down my legs.

I was afraid that if I allowed Benny to take it off me, I'd give in to him right there. I still planned to submit to him, but I wanted to buy a little more time.

Balling my thong up into a soggy ball of silk, I lobbed it in Benny's direction.

"Here, catch." I giggled.

He was close, only a few feet away, so snatching the garment out of the air was easy for him.

Lobbing the silk ball from one hand to the other, he said in a low voice, "What do you want to do now, Eliza?"

Oh, the things I wanted to do…to him…and him to me. He saw it in my eyes, so there was no point in pretending.

"I want you to do sinful things to me, Benny."

"That"—he edged closer and closer—"can be arranged. Whatever sinful things you're thinking of, I guarantee I can top 'em."

"You think so?"

He laughed. "Oh, I know I can."

"Benny…"

We swam to one another then, like we were in some corny movie. Only this was real life, and it felt anything but corny.

When his lips crashed down to mine, I savored how right it felt. I'd known since I'd hung that team pic on my wall, way back in the summer, that this day would come.

Or at least, I hoped it would.

Benny cupped my ass and lifted me up to him. I straddled his waist and slid down till I could feel *all* of him.

"I want you," I murmured.

It was the truth. I had to have him, in some way.

"Fuck, I want you, too," he growled.

I was dizzy with lust as we made out in the water. His cock kept bobbing and twitching against my clit as we moved together—rubbing, touching, feeling. I wanted more so I wiggled around until the head of him pushed at my entrance.

He pulled back. "Whoa, Eliza, hold up."

"Why?" I asked.

Our eyes met. He was giving me a chance to reconsider. In case this was moving too fast. Maybe it was, shit. I'd promised myself I wouldn't do this again, but I couldn't freaking think straight.

Lust had taken over, prompting me to ask, "Do you have a condom?"

I was on birth control, but I hadn't forgotten Lainey's warning that Benny was a player. *Better safe than sorry.* Not to mention, ending up pregnant once had made me a believer in extra protection.

He jerked his head toward his huge house. "I have a whole box of them in there. I can run in and get some."

I liked that he'd said "some." That meant I'd have him more than once. But I didn't feel like taking a time-out and have it ruin the mood.

Plus, maybe we *were* moving too fast. Now that we weren't all over each other, I could think more clearly. And I was having second thoughts. I had such a bad habit of getting caught up in the moment. That, of course, hadn't always worked out so well.

Is fucking him right away really a good idea?

We've only had this one freaking date.

Probably not the best move if I want him to take me seriously. He's already a man used to having women throw themselves at him.

Slow down, Eliza.

I looked at the rippling water, moonlit midnight blue in the night.

Benny, sensing my reticence, asked, "Is something wrong?"

I was honest. "I just think maybe we're moving too fast."

He sighed. "I understand you feeling that way, Eliza."

Could this guy get any sweeter?

Or sexier, I thought when he lowered the one hand that had been on my ass to touch my pussy.

"Oh-my-God-Benny," I murmured as he dipped two fingers inside me. "That feels sooo good."

It did. He was so damn skilled.

"See," he whispered in my ear, "there are other things we can do. I can fuck you with my fingers like this…"

He twisted just so, and, *fuuuck*, he hit that sensitive bundle of nerves.

I writhed against him, begging for more. "Yes, just like that. Right there, keep touching me. Please don't stop."

"I don't intend to stop, Eliza. Not until you fall apart."

"Yes," I gasped, my breasts rubbing against his firm chest. I glanced down and loved how my skin looked so milky and white in comparison to the dark ink of his tattoos. I was also relieved to see I wasn't leaking. How would I explain that?

Dispersing that worry, I reached down to stroke his rigid cock.

That put a little space between us…and kept him distracted with lust.

I was feeling pretty lusty myself and blurted out, "I want to taste you, Benny."

"Fuck, Eliza. Are you trying to kill me here?"

"No," I assured him as I traced the rim of his cock. "I just really want to make you feel as good as you're making me feel."

He lifted me up to the side of the pool, and I asked, "What are you doing? I thought you weren't going to stop?"

"I'm not. And I like what you just suggested. We'll definitely get to that. But first I'm going to taste you. Lean back on your elbows, beautiful," he murmured. "Watch me make you come."

"Oh, Benny…"

I did as he asked, and he parted my legs. I couldn't watch, though. Not yet. I just wanted to *feel*.

There was nothing at first, just the chill of the night on my openness. But then I felt his heated breaths…and the softness of his tongue.

"Yes."

I finally took a peek. He wanted me to watch, and I did so now. I watched until he shattered me into a million pieces.

I thought he was done with me. But Benny slid his fingers into me, moving and twisting until all I could do was work myself on him shamelessly till I fell apart again.

I was dizzy and weak by then, and I almost fell back. "No more," I gasped.

I tried to push him away. Well, kind of, but not really.

Holding me in place, he chuckled and said, "We're not done yet, Eliza. I think you have one more in you."

He was right, I did.

Spent at last, I laid back. But I soon mustered up some energy.

After all, I hadn't done anything for him. Plus, I'd made a promise I intended to keep.

Sliding back into the pool, I crooked a finger toward the shallow end. "Follow me, Benny."

He did. Oh, he did.

When we reached the shallow water, I turned to him and knelt. His cock was already hard, but he stroked it a few times until it was positively rigid.

When he touched the tip to my lips, I licked and kissed. And then I took all of him in my mouth. When he was close, I felt him tightening. He tried to pull back, but I grabbed his ass to hold him in place. Not that he put up any real struggle.

As I swallowed everything he gave me, he groaned, "Fuck, Eliza, fuck."

Afterward, we cleansed away the remains of our lusty encounter in the warm pool water.

We languished for awhile, sated and happy, floating around on a big raft he'd pulled into the water.

We talked late into the night, with Benny remaining as attentive as before we'd sexed things up.

Still, I felt a creep of worry.

Had we moved too fast?

Even though we'd not had full-on sex, we'd done enough that it made me question if I'd just become another notch on Benny's belt.

8

IF IT'S GOOD ENOUGH FOR YOU

BENNY

had no plans to blow off Eliza, but she seemed worried I would. I sensed it in the pool after we'd messed around and then again the day after when I called her. I asked her what was wrong, and she flat-out declared we'd moved too fast.

"What?" I said, thinking I'd heard her wrong. I mean, shit, it had all felt so good…and so fucking right.

"I just wished we'd waited," she reiterated with a sigh.

Nope, hadn't heard her wrong.

"Well, I don't wish that," I retorted, confused as fuck. "Everything we did felt amazing. Or am I wrong, Eliza?"

"You're not wrong. It was great. I just hope you don't think any differently about me now."

What does she think this is, 1947?

"Not at all," I assured her.

She seemed completely unconvinced, which made me wonder if she'd moved too fast with someone in her past and they'd ghosted her or something. I couldn't say I'd never done that to a woman. Hell, I had, like, repeatedly. But I wasn't planning on ghosting *her*. There was just something about Eliza, something that made me want to stick around to see where this burgeoning relationship could lead.

Oh, hell.

I couldn't believe I was thinking crap like that. I'd never been into any other woman like this. But Eliza, she was different. And I couldn't wait to see her again. I was sad our plan to go dancing was still a few nights away. But I couldn't move it up. I had an away game the next day against the LA Kings.

Cognizant of Eliza's fear that I was going to dump her, once I was out of town, I made sure to text and call her a shit ton of times. I did other things, too, like send her funny hockey memes. I even shared a few inside jokes about the players.

Brent is so superstitious, I texted her before the game.

We were all sitting around the locker room, waiting for some sage before-game words from Coach T.

How is he superstitious? Eliza wanted to know.

For one, he doesn't like anyone to touch his sticks before we hit the ice.

That doesn't sound too crazy.

Yeah, but I think I'm gonna fuck with him. I'm reaching over now to caress one. This should really work him up.

I wasn't really doing it, but Eliza's next text sounded so adamant that I didn't dare.

Noooo! Don't do it, Benny. What if he's onto something and you mess with the good hockey juju? You guys could lose the game!

Shit, she was right.

Good thing I'd never had any intention of touching Brent's sticks. To do so could indeed incur the wrath of the hockey gods. No fucking way did I want that on my conscience.

It warmed my heart to no end to have discovered sweet Eliza felt the same way.

I'd never actually do it, I assured her. *I was just messing with you.*

Coach came in then. *Oh, crap, gotta go. Your dad is about to start his pregame pep talk.*

Okay. Go kick some Kings's ass.

Will do.

See you soon.

You know it.

Can't wait for dancing.

Me, too.

Coach T gave his speech, and we hit the ice.

We lost that game, which totally sucked. Losing always did. And damn if I wasn't legit worried then that I'd somehow jinxed us, just by *joking* about angering the hockey gods.

One thing for sure—I'd never do that again.

Despite the loss, I was feeling good about returning to Las Vegas. I was so damn ready to see Eliza again. And though I wasn't much of a dancer, I planned to give it my all for her sake.

One thing I absolutely wouldn't be doing, however, was sharing any details of my clubbing past. Like how the guys and I used to hang around at the bar and wait for girls to flock to us, which they always did.

My MO used to be to choose whichever one struck my fancy. I'd focus on her, and it usually led to fucking her in the club restroom or in the back of her car.

But that was the past. I was looking solely to the future these days.

I'd picked that up at a recent meeting and found it to be a good philosophy to follow.

The only thing bothering me now was that Eliza was once again insisting on meeting me out.

"It'll be too busy in the club," I countered. "I might never find you. Just let me pick you up."

"No, that's okay. I can meet you out in the parking lot."

Fuck that. Not this time.

When date night arrived, I ignored all her texts asking when we should meet. I got in my car and drove straight to her house. I wasn't stupid about it, I'd gotten some info first, like last time.

Eliza's mom was out. Eliza herself had said as much in a text. Good, that meant she wouldn't be a factor. As for Eliza's dad, I learned—again from Dylan Culderway, who had to be wondering why I kept asking about Coach—that he'd be in his office late, just like before.

Perfect.

In case any of my info was bad, I decided to park a few houses down from Eliza's.

At her front door, I rang the doorbell. And then I stepped back and waited, hoping she wouldn't be too pissed at me for showing up unannounced.

When she opened the door, she did so just a crack, like she was hiding something.

"Benny," she exclaimed, looking not only shocked, but worried, as well.

Huh?

"Surprise," I said. "Sorry to show up when you're still getting ready"—she was wearing a short pink robe, and though her makeup was done, her hair was up in those hot roller things—"but, well… Here I am."

"We were supposed to meet in the club parking lot. Why'd you come to my house?"

"Hell with meeting in a stupid lot," I countered. "I wanted to pick you up on a proper date. Is that a problem?"

"I don't know," she inexplicably retorted.

"We're safe, babe, if that's what you're worried about. Your mom's still out, right?"

She nodded, and I shared with her, "Well, I have it on good word that your dad's down at the arena reviewing game footage. You know that takes hours."

"It does," she concurred.

I smiled. "So we're good?"

Sighing heavily, she glanced back over her shoulder, while still keeping the door semi-closed. *Weird.*

"Yeah," she said, at last, "I guess we are."

I tried to peer past her to see what she was hiding, and as I did I joked, "You don't have a secret boyfriend in there, do you?"

Shit, what if she says yes.

I knew then and there that it'd kill me. Fuck, I liked her way too much.

Luckily, she snorted, "Benny, don't be silly."

I wasn't trying to be *silly*, but for the life of me I couldn't imagine why she was acting so uneasy about me showing up. I mean, shit, her parents were fucking out.

And if there was no secret boyfriend, something I believed to be true, who else could be at her house that she wouldn't want me to see?

It was a true mystery. One that deepened when, glancing over her shoulder again, she murmured, "Uh, would you mind waiting out here for a few minutes? I need to straighten up a bit before I let you in." She laughed nervously. "We Townsends are a messy bunch."

I called bullshit. "Wow, really? Your dad is a total neat freak when it comes to his office."

Softly, eyes down, she said something that had me even more perplexed. "You never know what someone could be hiding, Benny. Appearances can be deceiving."

Huh? That seemed…odd. Were we talking about her dad, or was something else at play here?

What was Eliza not telling me?

From what little I could see past her body jammed in the doorway, the place didn't appear messy at all.

I knew then there was more to this secrecy crap. What could it be, though?

With a sigh, I relented. "Sure, I can wait out here."

She closed the door, and returned about ten minutes later. The first thing I noticed was that she'd lost the robe. She was now wearing a short black sequin dress, perfect for clubbing.

I could hardly keep my eyes off her. She just mesmerized me like that. As a result, I began to forget all about Eliza's weird behavior. She looked that damn stunning.

The little dress clung to her, and with the curlers out of her hair, her reddish-blonde mane flowed enticingly down her back.

I liked it.

And I liked the way her hips swayed when she led me through the foyer—all neat and tidy, by the way.

We then stepped down into a great room, and I finally tore my gaze from her to check around.

There was a huge sectional sofa and a stone fireplace that took up the entire back wall. That was really all I had time, or inclination, to take in.

Focusing back on Eliza, I murmured, "You look exceptionally beautiful tonight. Dressing up really suits you."

"It does you, too, Benny." She nodded to my sleek dark suit.

I wasn't nearly as close to perfection as she was, and I told her as much. "I could never look as amazing as you do right now, Eliza."

She turned the cutest shade of pink, making the sprinkle of freckles across the bridge of her nose stand out.

"That's sweet of you to say," she murmured, and then, clearing her throat, she made a motion to what looked to be the kitchen. "Are you thirsty at all? Would you like something to drink before we leave for the club?"

"Sure. A glass of water would be great."

"Bottled okay?"

"That's even better."

Eliza left the room, and I sat down on the big sectional sofa. Incidentally, the place looked neat as a pin.

Except for one thing…

Something had caught my eye—a small, pink plastic object, sticking out from between the sofa cushions.

Just as I was reaching for the mystery item, Eliza returned.

"Oh, wait, no!" she exclaimed, nearly dropping the water as she raced over to me.

Stymied, I froze. "What? What's wrong?"

She practically threw the bottled water my way. Luckily, I caught it with one hand. And then, just as she was lunging for the pink plastic whatever-it-was was that wedged in the cushions, I decided to go for it myself.

I mean, shit, I needed to see what it was if it had her in this much of a tizzy.

I was faster, of course, and got to it first.

"What is this thing?" I murmured as I lifted and held up the pink object for a more thorough inspection.

"Um, Benny, it's not what it looks like."

Oh, but it was, and I declared as much.

"This is one of those baby pacifier things."

With amazing speed—making me think maybe she should be on our team—Eliza snatched the item from my hand and swiftly tossed it into a drawer in the coffee table.

I looked at her like what-the-hell-was-that-about?

She just shrugged in return.

"What was that thing?" I asked, though I knew what it was and had said as much. "A baby pacifier, right," I reiterated.

"It was nothing," she said, looking away.

"Bullshit," I murmured.

My sister had had a baby not that long ago, and I knew what the hell pacifiers looked like. But that begged the question—why would there be a freaking baby pacifier at Coach's house? I knew for sure there were no little ones here, as Eliza was his only kid.

Maybe Mrs. Townsend babysits for someone? Or maybe Eliza does?

I was thinking of asking her about those possibilities, but then she blurted out, "Okay, yes, it's a baby pacifier, Benny. It belongs to me, okay? Like, for my personal use."

"What?" More confusion ensued. "What does that even mean?"

"It *means* the pacifier is mine. That's why it's pink. You know, because I'm a girl and all."

Uh-oh, maybe Eliza was a little touched.

Well, touched or not, I could work with this. That's right. If Eliza Townsend had an oral fixation that needed fulfilling, I had something *way* better than a pacifier she could put in her mouth.

I was about to say as much since we'd already gone *there*, but she began rambling, offering up a wacky, expanded explanation.

"The pacifier is part of that baby food diet I was telling you about in the grocery store. You remember that day, right? I had all that baby food in my cart."

I was still stuck on the pacifier being hers, so I just stared at her blankly.

"Pureed sweet potatoes?" she went on. "Ring a bell?"

I remembered just fine, and I finally said, "Yes, of course I remember."

Without a doubt, Eliza had a few screws loose. I'd never heard of that crazy baby food diet, but she sure was rigorously committed to it. Though, when all was said and done, I kind of had to admire a trait like that.

Eliza was still talking, and I tuned back in, in time to catch, "The pacifier is an integral part of the baby food diet program."

"It is, eh?" I raised a brow. This I had to hear. "How so?"

"Well"—I swear she was making this up as she went along—"when you're hungry, you pop the pacifier into your mouth. You then chew on it or whatever. That action gives you a feeling like you're eating something."

It was a stretch but I had to say, in a weird way, it all made sense. And that led me to ask, "Does it work?"

She made a big show of nodding. "Oh, yes, absolutely."

It was bizarre, sure, but my teammates had tried crazier diets and wackier regimens than that. I often overheard them talking about tricks and tips to reach a certain weight goal, or shit you could do to up your fitness quotient.

That right there made my next words possible. "Hey, maybe I should try it."

Eliza looked horrified, even as she calmly replied, "Yeah, sure. I guess you could give it a shot."

"It might help with my donut addiction," I replied.

She cocked her head. "I didn't know you had a donut addiction. I did see donuts in your cart at the store, but I thought nothing of it."

Sheepishly, I replied, "Yeah, well, you should have. I *have* a donut addiction, Eliza, not had. Please don't tell your dad, though. I'm working on it, I swear. Besides, he might be more pissed about the donuts than us going out."

"I doubt that," she scoffed. "But don't worry. My lips are sealed."

"Thanks. So about that pacifier... Do you mind if we stop at Target on the way to the club? I'd like to buy one and give it a try."

She gave me another funny look but agreed.

Though I was onboard with the pacifier aspect of the crazy baby food plan, I was quick to declare, "I'm drawing the line at eating pureed sweet potatoes, though."

She raised a brow. "Oh, you are? What about the dessert we had? You seemed to enjoy that."

"It's one thing for the sweet potatoes to be hidden away in a sugar-laden tart. But fuck that baby food slop."

Upon hearing that, she genuinely laughed.

9

PUCK BUNNY WHAT?

ELIZA

Oh God, poor Benny. He believed my nutty, on-the-fly explanation as to why there had been a pacifier stuck between the cushions of our family sofa.

Why I hadn't simply said it belonged to someone's baby—other than my own, of course—was beyond me.

I suppose I was too worried if I ascribed the object to an actual infant, Benny might somehow put the pieces together that *I* was the only one in my small circle of acquaintances who could have a child.

Ugh, keeping Ava a secret was taking on a life of its own.

And that wasn't good.

The longer I waited to spill the beans, the more I had no idea how to do it. People were going to be pissed that I waited so long to come clean. People like my friend Lainey…and people like Benny.

Hell, he'd probably end up hating me forever.

I sure had boxed myself into a corner.

And that made me want to cry.

Even if Benny didn't dump me for keeping such a huge secret from him, this new diet farce was like adding fuel to the fire of my deceit. Once he discovered the baby food diet was a sham, he was sure to be less than thrilled he'd bought into it.

And he did just that on the way to the club. After a quick stop at the local Target, Benny had in his possession a brand-new pacifier. Blue… to go with mine that was pink.

Kill me now. Before Benny does.

I just thanked God he didn't put the damn thing in his mouth in front of me. I would've lost it on the spot.

Aw shit, the truth is sure to come out when he does that exact thing in front of a teammate.

Even if he didn't do that, Benny was sure to share this supposed diet with his friends.

What if they bought into it, too?

My dad would *not* find it amusing to have his players running around, chomping on freaking pacifiers. He'd wonder where they came up with the idea in the first place. Then my name would be brought up. My father would question how I even knew Benny, especially so well that I felt comfortable talking pacifiers and baby food with him.

That would then lead to a mention of Ava.

And I'd be busted.

So yeah, this fake diet could not get out to my father. I had to take action now.

As we drove to the club in Benny's sleek black Porsche, I casually said, "Could you do me a huge favor, Benny?"

He glanced over at me, no doubt curious as to what this "huge favor" could be.

"It's not that huge," I qualified.

"Huge or not, Eliza, ask away."

God, he was so sweet.

And I was such an ass.

Here goes nothing.

"Um, can you keep the pacifier stuff and the baby food diet on the down-low, at least for a little while?"

We were pulling up to the club by that point, and as we waited for the valet guy to come to us his brow furrowed.

"Yeah, sure, okay," he said.

The valet dude arrived and opened my door first. But before I got out of the car, I said, "It's just that my dad knows about this new diet of mine, and he'd definitely put together that I was the person who told you about it. That would totally out us."

"No problem, Eliza," he said. "The diet and pacifier will stay our little secret."

"Thank you, Benny."

Any further talk of pacifiers and baby food diets was mercifully shelved.

On our way into the club, Benny brought up the game they'd just played in LA, which was fine with me. Once we were past the bouncer checking IDs, however, the music grew far too loud to hold much of a conversation.

That was okay, too. The beat had me moving already. It'd been so long since I'd shaken my booty that I couldn't wait to hit the dance floor. I was vibrating with enthusiasm, and Benny laughed as he let me drag him along.

Under the lights, we danced and danced. I was no great dancer, but Benny was worse than me. He had some funny moves that made me laugh, but overall he sucked. Still, we had a blast. I could've stayed out there forever, but thirst eventually caught up with us.

"Do you mind if we head over to the bar?" I screamed to Benny over the pulsing music. "I'm parched."

"Sure," he yelled back. "I could go for some water."

I ordered a Diet Coke, and Benny asked for the water he wanted. We decided to stay at the bar to drink our beverages. It was a little quieter there and we could actually hear one another.

"Are you having fun, Eliza?" he asked once we were seated on stools.

Sipping on my soda, I nodded.

"Good," he said.

We chatted then about the music and such, but our conversation ground to a halt when some chick with big hair and even bigger boobs noticed Benny and made a beeline for him.

"Oh, great," he murmured sarcastically.

"A fan?" I said.

"Probably."

The bleached blonde sauntered up to my date, and shooting me a dismissive glance, purred to him, "Hey, Benny, imagine running into *you* here. It's been such a long time. Can I buy you a drink?"

Huh, I guess he knows her from the past.

"I don't drink anymore," he replied as he scanned her face, looking puzzled.

"Who is she?" I mouthed to him when her buzzing phone distracted her.

He shrugged and mouthed back, "I'm not sure."

Well, she clearly knew him.

When she was done with her phone, she went on to say, "You're not drinking anymore, huh? When I last saw you, you were sucking them down like nobody's business."

Laughing nervously, he raised his glass and said, "Ice-cold water is about as wild as I get these days."

"That's a shame," she remarked. "It sounds like life has gotten rather boring for you."

Benny frowned. "There's no shame in boring."

"Well, sometimes there is." Leaning in to him, she murmured, "But, as I recall, you sure weren't boring in bed."

"Hey!"

That was me, making my presence known, and going on to say, "I think it's time for you to move along, lady. This is a date we're on, you know. And contrary to how you're treating me, I'm not invisible."

She rolled her eyes, and I was ready to kick her ass—okay, maybe just threaten her a little—but Benny stepped between us to diffuse the situation.

"You should probably leave," he said to Blondie. "I don't know what you're talking about, anyway."

She was not deterred. "Oh, now don't be coy, Benny."

"Seriously, I don't know who you are."

Oh, she didn't like that. Huffing and puffing like a petulant child, she hissed, "You most certainly do know me, in many, many ways."

She stared him down, and when he still couldn't place her, she whined, "I'm Clarisse, damn it. We met about a year and a half ago at a party." She winked. "You remember me now, right?"

He had no clue who she was or what she was talking about. I knew that because he murmured, "Uh, I'm thinking here."

Oh, boy.

Hands on her hips, she said, "I can't believe you've forgotten all the things we did in the hot tu—"

"Hey there now," he interjected, cutting her off and glancing over at me sheepishly. "There's no need to go there. I think I remember you now."

Think? I rolled my eyes at him, and he looked away.

When his focus returned to Clarisse, it was like a light had suddenly turned on. I knew then that she was telling the truth. Benny, without a doubt, had slept with her. And done who knows what kind of kinkery in the hot tub.

Ugh!

I reminded myself that all that had occurred long before I'd met him, and also when he was way out of control. What bothered me, though, was that he had no recollection of the event. It had taken her prodding to jar whatever disjointed memory he had of her.

And that gave me pause.

Lainey had said Benny was a player, but witnessing the fallout— this girl—up close and personal left me cold.

Clarisse finally left, but to me, our night was done. We danced some more, but what she'd said was freaking bothered me.

Benny noticed I was off and asked if everything was okay. That was once we were away from the loud music, having retreated to a relatively quiet corner of the club.

"Yes, everything's fine," I said, not wanting to talk about it in a public place.

There was an awkward silence for a good five minutes, and then he said, "Do you just want to go home, Eliza? You look like you're not having much fun anymore."

Nodding, I conceded, "Yeah, we should leave."

I wanted to check in on Ava, anyway. When my mom had taken her out earlier, I'd been showering and hadn't had a chance to see her off.

The drive home was mostly quiet. When we pulled up to my house, I just wanted to make a quick getaway. Not only did I need some time to think about this thing with Benny, but my dad would be on his way home from the arena and could catch us.

My quick getaway was stalled, though, when Benny cut the ignition.

He leaned back in his seat and said, "You were so quiet the whole way home. Are you sure we're good, Eliza?"

"Yes." I nodded. "We're great."

He blew out a breath. "Okay, well, I have a long road trip coming up with the team, but once we get back I'd like to see you again. Maybe we could catch a movie, or go out for another night of dancing."

Manwhore or not, he was sweet. And he looked so handsome in the moonlit night. But I had to be strong. I was just too confused about him.

I opened the door, needing some air.

Steeling myself, I said, "Maybe we can do something. Just call or text me when you return. We can figure things out from there."

Sensing a brush-off, Benny placed his hand on my forearm. "Eliza, wait, please. Figure things out? What's that even mean?" I shrugged, and he said, "See, something is wrong."

I closed the door. We were going to talk, after all.

"I think I know what caused this," he quietly stated.

"No, no," I insisted, not wanting to kick off our talk with hot tub Clarisse. "Everything's cool. I just meant figure things out, as to where we should go on our next date."

"Right," he murmured sarcastically. "And if that's really true, then why are you saying things like I should call or text *after* I get back? What about while I'm away? Do you not want to hear from me?"

Softly, I admitted, "I don't know, Benny. Maybe not while you're away."

"I knew it."

"Benny, I just need some time to think."

He raked his hand through his long hair. "That damn girl at the club, she ruined everything. She freaked you out."

"It isn't *her* that's bothering me," I blurted out.

"What is it, then?"

"It's hard to explain."

"Can you try?"

I took a few breaths and then said, "I know you have a past, Benny. I'd expect you to. But you didn't even *remember* that you'd slept with that girl. That's just... I don't even know. But I know it's not good."

"I remembered her just fine," he protested. When I shot him a look, he amended, "So it took me a minute or two, so what?"

We were getting nowhere. "Okay, I'm out."

My hand was back on the door handle, but I hesitated when Benny said, "Eliza, please, don't run off. Talk to me, okay? In my meetings they say communication is always the key."

"That may be true," I conceded, "but I don't think there's anything more to say, not tonight."

"Sure there is. If there wasn't, it wouldn't feel like you're still pissed at me."

I looked down at my hands. "I actually don't know what I'm feeling right now. That's why I should just go in the house. All I know is, you going away will be good for us."

"How do you see that?" He sounded hurt.

"It'll give us some space."

"I don't need space, Eliza."

"Well, I do."

Scrubbing his hand down his face, he said, "I'm sorry that girl came up to us, really I am. The truth is, I hate that no matter how hard I try to put my past behind me, I never can. It looked bad, I know, me not remembering Charisse and all."

"Uh, I think her name is *Cl*arisse."

"Shit, whatever."

We fell silent then, until Benny said, "Can I just say one more thing?"

"Yes, of course."

I may have been upset, but I didn't want to end things with him right there. Really, we were just getting started. And it'd been such a good start. I wanted to get past this, so maybe letting him open up was a good thing, after all.

My conscience chimed in with a hearty laugh. *Ha, you're one to be casting aspersions, Eliza.*

I'd deal with that later. Right now we were focused on Benny, who was currently exhaling slowly, gearing up to say, "You didn't know me before, and I'm not gonna lie. I was a real prick."

"You mean regarding your behavior with women?" I clarified.

"Yes, that's what I mean. But there were other problems, too. Problems I've since addressed. As you know, drinking was huge for me."

Curious to know what other demons Benny had fought, I asked, "Were there drugs?"

"Not a lot, but sometimes."

Damn. "Shit, Benny."

"That's all behind me, Eliza. You know I went to rehab last fall. And you also know I go to meetings to keep my shit together."

I knew all that, but I had to ask, "What about the women issue? What have you done about that?"

"I think I've gotten that under control."

"*Think*, Benny...or you have?"

"I have."

He didn't sound so sure, but I left it at that. As in, I actually started getting out of his car.

I stopped only to reiterate for him not to call or text till he got back.

Though I tried to lessen the sting by adding, "I promise we can talk more about all this when you return. I just need some time to process things."

It was true. I did need time, but not just for me. I had to rethink this whole thing for Ava's sake.

Shit, I needed to tell him about her, especially if things progressed any further. That was why I had to be one-hundred percent sure Benny was real relationship material, not just a guy meant for fun.

Like I'd told him, I was glad he had a string of road games coming up. I'd seen them on the schedule and knew they were all up in western Canada. I'd have ample time to assess the situation thoroughly with him so far away. Maybe I'd also have a chance to talk with Lainey about this whole mess. She might have some insight.

That chance came a few days later. But what a surprise I received. To say her reaction was lukewarm at best would have been an understatement.

I'd truly thought Lainey was rooting for me and Benny to get together. She'd said as much, but I guess she'd changed her mind. When I talked with her, she discouraged me from pursuing anything with Benny, even going so far as to inform me he kept a directory of puck bunnies.

"Like, for booty calls," she said.

Yuck.

On top of the Clarisse incident, this was huge. I definitely needed time to think. I couldn't date that big of a dog. Ava deserved better role models for the future. She was a baby right now, but I needed to get in the habit of making wise choices regarding the people I put in her life.

But before I dismissed Benny the Player completely, I decided to give him one last chance. An opportunity, if you will, to prove he was a changed man.

I knew just how to do it, too. I came up with a "test."

But first, I needed to get my hands on that damn puck bunny directory.

10

I'LL BUY THE MATCHES

BENNY

I spent most of the road trip worried about Eliza, worried about stupid puck bunnies, and worried even more about stupid me. I needed to show the girl who was turning my life upside down that I'd changed.

How in the hell was I supposed to do that?

I thought I'd done a pretty good job of brushing off the puck bunny that had approached us at the club. Whatever. I just should've leveled with Eliza from the start, confessed how bad I once was.

Then I could've let her in on how much I'd changed, and how she'd had a role, as of late, in curbing my womanizing ways.

I'd do all that when I returned to Vegas, but for now, I needed to focus on the upcoming road games.

So focus I did.

I was successful at keeping my mind on hockey during the first game of the trip. We were playing the Vancouver Canucks, and I was one hundred percent in the game. I played extremely well, putting up two assists and scoring one goal. And that was just in the second period.

My linemates, Brent and Nolan, wondered what had gotten into me.

"You were on fire out there, Benny," Brent remarked when we were back in the locker room between periods.

Nolan, seated on a bench in the stall next to me, chimed in with, "Yeah, whatever's gotten into you, keep it up. We're down by one"—despite my second-period blitz, the score was four to three Canucks—"but if we all play as hard as you've been playing, we got this one in the bag."

We did play as hard, if not harder than I had, in the third, and won the game by a final score of six to four. After the game, Coach Townsend had only kind words for me in the locker room.

"Excellent game, Perry," he said with a rare smile directed at me. "That's the kind of work ethic I like to see."

I decided then and there I was going to keep it up. Plus, from here on out I planned to fight just as hard to keep Eliza.

I legit had to wonder if Coach would say the same thing if he knew I'd be putting his work ethic words to use to win back his daughter's trust.

Then again, maybe he wouldn't be so opposed.

I had a feeling Coach could be turned around with the right incentive, maybe even by a man who had nothing but good intentions toward his daughter. He'd issued his stay-away-from-Eliza edict expressly to prevent players from using her. *I* really cared. Of course, all this rah-rah Coach stuff was predicated on if Eliza still wanted me in her life.

Fuck!

I hated that she'd asked me not to communicate with her throughout this trip. How was I supposed to worm my way back into her good graces? I'd need to do something once I got back. But what? How could I make her believe in me again?

By the time we made it to Calgary, the next game site, I was a complete wreck.

But then I had an idea...

Though I couldn't call or text the woman messing with my mind, I *could* share my jumbled thoughts with someone who might help keep me sane till we returned to Vegas.

Unfortunately, my usual go-to bros, Brent and Nolan, were not options. Those two were just too in love these days—Brent with Aubrey, and Nolan with Lainey. They'd be of no help.

What I needed was some clear, objective advice. The only man I could think of to give me that was Dylan Culderway.

So Dylan it was.

After an early morning practice at the Saddledome in Calgary, I asked if he'd be up for grabbing a quick cup of coffee.

"Sure, man. What's up?" he said.

He'd already caught on to the fact that this was more than an invitation for a routine caffeine run.

Oh, hell, I just laid it on the line. "I was hoping to run some stuff past you. Get your opinion on things."

"What? Like hockey things?"

"No," I confessed. "More like personal crap."

"You got it," he said. "I'm no expert, but I'll help if I can."

He was a stand-up dude and I knew I'd made the right decision to go to him.

There was a coffee shop close to the arena, so we decided to just walk down to it. Too bad for us it was snowing like hell and cold as fuck. By the time we reached our destination, he and I were a human Popsicles.

"Shit, dude,"—I shook a plume of snow from my long woolen coat—"I forgot how fucking cold it gets up here."

"It does," Dylan agreed, chuckling. "I grew up in Buffalo, though, so I don't really mind." He looked thoughtful as he paused, then added, "I actually really love weather like this."

I pointed at him. "You, my friend, are fucked in the head."

"Only about as much as you are, Perry."

Snorting, I agreed, "You're right about that one."

I clapped him on the back and a cloud of snow puffed off his coat like it had mine. "Now let's go grab that coffee and warm the fuck up," I said.

A few minutes later, we were loaded up with piping-hot mugs of brew. We had settled in by a big window at the front of the store. Dylan, who was almost as perceptive as the great sensei, Nolan, gave me a knowing look before I even opened my mouth to start the conversation.

"Oh, shit, here we go," I said. "I wear my heart on my sleeve, don't I?"

"You do, Benny, but it's not just that that gives you away. From the way you've been acting all wound up tight lately, this personal stuff you want to talk about *has* to involve a woman."

He was so right. "Does it ever," I said, laughing. "Is it really that obvious, though?"

"Yeah, pretty much."

"Crap."

Since there was no point in getting into anything till he knew the *whole* story, which including the fact my woman trouble had to do with a very specific off-limits girl, I readied myself to fill him in. He already knew I was seeing someone on the sly; he just didn't know who it happened to be.

It was time he learned the truth, so, blowing out a breath, I blurted out, "I'm dating Coach's daughter."

Dylan almost choked on his coffee.

"You're shitting me, right?" he said once he recovered.

"I wish I were, but I'm not."

"Damn, Benny. You really do have a self-destructive streak."

I raised my cup. "My motto in life does seem to be 'go big or go home.'"

"You got the 'go home' part right," he snorted. "Once Coach T finds out you're nailing his daughter, he'll be sending you back to Surrey in a pine box."

"That'd be pretty pathetic, Dylan, seeing as I haven't even gotten to the nailing-his-daughter part yet."

He looked shocked. "Wow. This one really must mean something to you."

"She does."

He raised a brow. "Maybe that's the real problem?"

"Nah, not in the way you're thinking." I sighed and leaned back. "I don't mind liking her this much. I mean, I did at first, but not now. I've come to my senses and have finally realized I *need* a girl like Eliza in my life. She's fun and I like her. I want this to work, damn it."

"I'm not seeing a problem here, dude."

"Oh, there is. Trust me, there is."

"Like what?"

"For one, Eliza and I ran into some puck bunny I once fucked when we were out on a goddamn date."

Dylan winced, and I said, "I know, right? Eliza was *not* happy about it. So, see, there's one problem right there."

"Hey, it was just bad luck that you ran into that girl. It'll probably never happen again. Work this out with Eliza and forget about it."

"Dude"—I gave him a look—"it's not that simple. There are *so* many more women we could potentially run into."

"Fuck. That could be a problem."

"Yeah, see. That one alone spooked Eliza. I could see it happening again and again, and her being mad over and over. This is assuming she takes me back. I really don't know if she will. She was super pissed that it took me a while to remember the girl at the club."

"Benny, really dude? You're telling me you couldn't remember a girl you once fucked?"

"I really couldn't," I admitted. "It's actually still a little fuzzy."

He shook his head. "Wow, man. Just...wow."

"Yeah, yeah, I know. I was a pig in the past. But what can I do about it now?"

He shrugged, and I let him in on the part that was driving me nuts.

"Before this trip, Eliza told me not to contact her. She needs"—I made air quotes—"time to think."

Dylan made a face. "That doesn't sound good. Not good at all."

"I know. I think she's seriously considering kicking me to the curb, like, permanently."

"And you don't want that to happen?"

"No way. We only just started dating. I don't want it to end already."

Dylan thought for a minute, and then said, "Then show her how much you've changed."

I snorted, "How in the hell do I do that?"

He leaned back and crossed his arms over his chest. "That is a tough one. Maybe just try showing her by your actions."

"If she ever gives me a chance," I lamented.

"Make *sure* you get a chance."

"That's easier said than done."

"Not really. I'm sure Eliza, like most women, just wants to be able to trust you. She'll give you that chance once she does."

"Okay, great. So how do I get her to trust me?"

"Start by being upfront with her. You're gonna have to tell her *everything*."

"*Every*thing?" I swallowed hard. "Should I even fill her in on the existence of the infamous puck bunny directory?"

Dylan didn't look surprised. He obviously had heard about my directory. Seemed everyone had, except Eliza.

"Sure," he said. "After her initial anger wears off—and trust me, she's going to be *pissed* you have a directory of chicks you bang—you two can hash it out. Maybe you could do something symbolic, like burn the damn thing together."

"I like that," I said.

It was amazing. A month before, Dylan's advice would've sounded blasphemous. But with how I felt about Eliza and how much I wanted things to work out, I was ready to go buy the damn matches.

11

CLOWNIE, MY NEW CONFIDANTE

ELIZA

Luckily for me *and* the implementation of my ingenious plan, Benny diverted from our "no contact till he returned" agreement. Just a few days before he was set to return, he called to ask me if I could feed his fish.

"I'm sorry to bother you, Eliza," he said after he explained the fish-in-need-of-food situation. "I have a housekeeper that takes care of these things when I'm out of town. But an emergency came up for her, and she can't make it these next few days."

"It's not a problem, Benny," I assured him. "I understand. I promise I won't let your little buddies starve."

"Thanks, Eliza," I imagined him smiling from the kind tone of his voice. "You're the best."

I didn't know what to say to that, but I did have a question. "Uh, how do I get in to your house?"

He laughed. "I guess a key would help, eh?"

"It would."

"Don't worry. There's one under the planter by the garages."

"Got it," I replied.

"Thank you, again," Benny said, and then in the sweetest, most heartfelt tone, he murmured, "The fishes and I owe you a night out on the town once I get back."

I wasn't sure how to respond, as I was still up in the air on the future of me and him. One dinner wouldn't hurt, though, would it? Ah, crap, I so wanted to forgive him.

"Okay," I conceded. "That sounds nice."

"Great. But not a seafood place, all right? My gilled friends would frown on that."

I couldn't help but laugh. Benny had an uncanny ability to make me smile, even when I felt unsure about him.

Damn it, I wanted things to work out. Despite my misgivings, I really missed Benny. All I needed to move forward was to know that his player days were truly done. Then we'd be fine. I could tell him about Ava and everything.

That's why I had devised a plan, or a "test," if you will.

And now, thanks to Benny's fish needing nourishment, I could make it happen. The unexpected access to his house gave me a perfect opportunity to find the nefarious puck bunny directory. That would kick-start my covert operation to give Benny a chance to prove he'd changed.

I hoped he had.

I wanted him to pass the test...and soon.

That rush prompted me to begin my search for the directory

the very first day I went over to feed what I assumed would be a few guppies.

Wow, was I ever wrong on the fish front.

Benny had what could only be described as a mini ocean in his living room. The massive aquarium took up one whole wall, and inside were fish of all shapes, sizes, and colors, swimming merrily about.

I sprinkled fish food in their tank and watched as they got caught up in a feeding frenzy.

My mind was pretty frenzied, as well, as I wracked my brain, asking, *where would a guy like Benny hide his directory of easy lays*?

"Where do you guys think it is?" I asked the occupants of the tank.

They, not surprisingly, ignored me.

Except for one brightly colored orange and white fish.

"I think you're a clownfish," I mused.

I checked my phone.

Yep, he was.

The little fish was as comical as his name. He juked and jived, and then just kind of hung there staring at me.

I laughed and assured him, "I promise when I let Benny take me out to a restaurant, it absolutely will not be a seafood place."

I swear his little scaly brows went up.

"Hey, hey, don't worry. We may not even be going if Benny doesn't pass the test I have planned for him."

I proceeded to share with the clownfish, who remained at the front of the tank, my whole brilliant plan.

I then resumed wondering where the puck bunny directory could be.

"The bedroom seems like a good place to start, right?" I asked the fish.

Okay, I was really losing it. A fact made crystal clear when my new bud, cute as all get-out, peered out at me from his watery abode with his little mouth working overtime and his fish lips mouthing, "Don't do it, don't do it!"

He knew what I was about to do and was trying to stop me. Or maybe, and this was the more likely explanation, my guilty conscience was speaking to me through the fish. Then again, it could've been something altogether different weighing on my mind.

"Yeah, like not telling Benny I have a child."

Clownfish, who I christened Clownie in that moment, looked appalled to hear of my deception.

"I know, I know," I said. "I can't keep Ava a secret forever. And hard or not, I'm going to tell Benny. First, though, I need to know if he's worth it. *That's* why I have to find that stupid directory as soon as possible."

"Snooping is wrong," I imagined Clownie retorting. He looked like a judge-y fish, after all.

I snorted. "That's easy for you to say. You're a fish."

"Ah, and that's where you're mistaken. I'm a very wise old fish. And you, my human friend, are very clearly a stupid young woman."

"Hey!"

"You claim you're worried that you can't trust Benny, yet you harbor a huge secret of your own."

"Cute, I get it. Harbor…fish. I see what you're trying to do. Funny."

"Stay focused, human."

"I am focused, fish."

It hit me then, the absurdity of having an imaginary discussion with a freaking fish! Oh, hell, I was simply hashing out what I was mulling over in my mind. I felt so damn guilty for setting up a test for

Benny while I kept a secret of my own.

"This can't go on," I whispered to Clownie.

"No, it can't," I pretended he replied, while in reality, he'd already swam away.

I didn't want Benny to swim away, too. So I decided no matter the consequences, I'd tell him about my daughter...right after he passed the test.

Finding the directory was easy. It wasn't even discreetly hidden. I located the innocuous-looking red spiral-bound notebook during my first round of snooping. The dreaded puck bunny directory had been tucked away in a nightstand drawer in Benny's bedroom.

I sat on the edge of his bed and opened the damn thing, preparing for the worst.

But as I flipped through the pages, I felt kind of relieved.

There weren't nearly as many entries as I feared there would be. Plus, most were girls living in other cities. I knew this because Benny had jotted down last-known addresses next to names and numbers.

"A girl in every port," I murmured, sighing. "Men can be such pigs sometimes."

Benny obviously was no exception to that observation.

But he'd changed, or so he claimed. "We shall see," I murmured.

As I neared the back of the book, I came upon the entry for Clarisse, the blonde from the club. It had to be her, right? How many women could there be in the book named Clarisse?

I wasn't mad, I was elated. I'd been counting on finding her in the directory. *She* was the key to implementing my plan.

I just hoped she'd go along with it.

I read her entry and noted Benny had a rating system. He'd given Clarisse four stars. *How lovely.* We sure had a lot to talk about, that man and I.

I went back downstairs, directory in hand, and sat next to my new friend, Clownie.

Don't judge. I needed the moral support from something breathing, even if it was through gills.

I needed that support because what I did next was pick up my phone and call Clarisse.

After I explained who I was, the girl who'd been with Benny at the club, I cleared my throat and said, "I guess you're wondering why I'm calling?"

"I am curious," she replied.

"This may sound weird, but I have this plan I'm working on. And I really need *your* help to make it happen."

She hadn't hung up on me yet, so that was a plus.

"Hmm, this plan you're working on..." She sounded intrigued. *Yes!* "Does it involve Benny?"

"It sure does."

"I may be interested, then."

Perfect, I thought.

But then I started reconsidering when she said, "Is this a sex thing? If it is, that's fine. Are you calling 'cause you want me to hook up with you and Benny?"

Yikes.

Quickly, before she got into specifics, I replied, "Good God, no. It's nothing like that."

"Aw, darn," she sighed. "I would've been up for a threesome, so long as it included him."

"Are you crazy?" I accidentally said out loud.

"I most certainly am not," she huffed. "And there's no need to sound so offended. You never know, you could end up having a good time if we all went to bed together."

Not happening!

I drew in a deep, calming breath, and then said, "I'm sorry for snapping at you. And I'm not offended. It's just that I really like Benny, and I don't want to share him with you or anyone else. That's actually why I need your help with the plan I mentioned."

"What is this stupid plan of yours, anyway?" She sounded like she was losing patience. "And how in the hell do I fit into it?"

Knowing it'd be better to fill her in on the details in person—that way she couldn't run away—I said, "Could we meet somewhere? I think it's better if I explain face-to-face."

"Oh, all right. I suppose we could meet. When and where are you thinking?"

I needed to move fast, so I said, "What about today?"

"Hmm, that could work. I do have some shopping I need to take care of. I'll be over at the mall in an hour or so."

"Which mall?" I asked.

As luck would have it, she was going to the mall closest to Benny's house.

"Perfect," I declared.

"Wanna meet at the food court at around two?"

"That works for me," I replied.

I ended the call before she could change her mind. Then I stood and did a little happy dance in front of the fish tank.

"Things are in motion," I sang out to Clownie. "I'm meeting Clarisse in an hour. Wish me luck. Let's hope she doesn't think I'm completely crazy once I tell her my plan. And let's pray she's a good sport about it."

"Glug, glug, glug," Clownie replied, blowing bubbles.

Chuckling at my fish friend, I scampered upstairs and placed the puck bunny directory back where I'd found it.

An hour later, I was at the mall and ready to meet Clarisse. I was thrilled to see she'd not backed out. She was at the food court, as planned. I spotted her right away at a corner table, sucking down a bright pink frappuccino.

She really was the perfect temptation for Benny. Her sexed-up look was just what was needed. Her blown-out, platinum hair and massive boobs, all on full display in a barely-there silky halter dress, were perfect.

I was nearly at her table when I looked down at my own chest and sighed. Benny was definitely a boob man. I had pretty big breasts, but Fake Boobs had me beat by a mile, or at least by a cup size.

When I reached the table, I introduced myself.

Clarisse kicked things off by apologizing for her behavior at the club, which I viewed as a good start.

"I was kind of drunk," she explained. "I didn't mean to be so bitchy to you."

"It's all right," I replied.

When I sat down across from her, she asked, "So why exactly am I here? What's this plan of yours that involves Benny? And, like I said on the phone, how do I fit into it?"

I was surprised she hadn't yet asked how I'd obtained her phone number. I guess she didn't care. And she sure seemed intrigued when I detailed my plan to her. I was certain to provide lots of details, so there'd be no miscommunications.

When I finished, I said, "So are you in?"

"Maybe…" She lifted her hand and peered down at her long, talon-like nails. "Depends on what's in it for me."

"Um, what do you mean?"

"Well, I'm not going along with a plan like that for nothing."

"Okay. What do you want?" I queried.

She tapped a bloodred nail to her chin and said, "If you promise to introduce me to a different Wolves player, I'm in. I'll do whatever you want then."

Oh, boy.

Her and the hockey players, she was worse than me.

But I needed her cooperation.

So I pondered, and the first player I came up with was Benny's good friend.

"Dylan Culderway," I exclaimed. "He's available from what I hear."

She liked the idea of Dylan, but then I panicked. I wasn't so sure he'd go for someone like her. I didn't know Dylan that well, but he seemed like a serious kind of guy. And Clarisse was anything but serious.

"Maybe Dylan's not such a good choice," I said, backtracking. "Let me think of someone else."

Too late, Clarisse was dead set on Dylan.

"I don't want anyone else," she whined. "Dylan Culderway is super hot. Plus…" She leaned across the table and whispered, "Defensemen, for some reason, are usually just so *big*."

She winked, and I had to ask, "You mean *big*, as in the overall build department?"

"Among other things," she murmured, sitting back.

Huh, interesting.

I was intrigued, but I was only into Benny. So I dropped the subject and got back to why we were meeting.

"We're good?" I said. "With the plan, that is."

"Sure. I'm good with it all. You want me to meet you in the mall parking lot this Tuesday, right?"

"Yes, this Tuesday. That's the day Benny returns."

With the details finalized for my test for Benny, I wrapped things up with Clarisse. She got up and left shortly thereafter, slurping on her pink frap.

I sat there alone in the food court, hoping like hell Benny would pass the upcoming test.

I was hoping even more that he wouldn't end up hating me for coming up with a test of his loyalty in the first place.

12

SURPRISE!

BENNY

Tuesday was the craziest day. We got back to Las Vegas and Dylan's car wouldn't start. It was a brand-new Ferrari, so go figure.

I stayed with him in the team parking lot at the airport till the service guy arrived, along with a flatbed tow truck. That didn't bode well for the fate of the car. Sure enough, the Ferrari needed more than what could be done by the service person on-site.

Since Dylan had no car to drive home, I offered him a ride.

"Thanks, man," he said. "I really appreciate it."

"Not a problem," I assured him.

We got in my Porsche—for which, as so eloquently stated in that cinematic classic *Risky Business*, there is no substitute.

Dylan, like he'd read my mind, remarked, "I should've bought one of these."

"You should've," I agreed.

My teammate lived on the opposite side of town, so I headed in that direction. I also soon learned he lived in the sugar-laden section of Las Vegas. *Jesus.* I swear we must've passed five donut shops before reaching his neighborhood.

I could've killed for a donut by then. I'd been successfully abstaining, but this level of temptation was just too much. I was about to cave.

I knew what I needed—my crutch, the baby pacifier. I could then stay strong in the face of what felt like a concerted effort by the donut gods to tempt me.

Should I take out my little blue helper?

I glanced over at Dylan. He seemed lost in thought, tapping along to a song that had just come on the radio. I doubted he'd notice, or even care, if I popped the pacifier into my mouth.

During our road game stint, I'd been extremely careful about keeping my hunger helper out of sight. But Dylan wasn't like a lot of the other guys. He stayed out of people's business—unless, of course, as I had done in Calgary, you asked him for his opinion.

So, feeling at ease, I went ahead and retrieved the pacifier from the console and popped it in my mouth.

Ahh, that's so much better.

I immediately relaxed. These things really were soothing as fuck. No wonder babies liked them so much.

I was wrong about Dylan, though. He started staring over at me like I'd lost my mind.

"What the fuck is that thing in your mouth?" he asked. "Is that a fucking baby pacifier?"

"Yeth," I garbled from around the rubbery nub.

He shook his head. "You, my man, have lost it."

I popped the pacifier out of my mouth. "Aw, fuck."

Tossing the damn thing back into the console, I tried to explain. "Look, I know this sounds weird, but it's an integral part of this new behavioral modification plan I'm trying, some new baby food diet craze."

"Baby food diet craze?" He appeared mystified, what with his crinkled brow and all.

"Yes," I stated confidently, "the pacifier works with this new baby food diet."

"Hmm, *I've* never heard of any baby food diet. And I've definitely never heard of a baby pacifier being part of *any* sort of behavioral modification regimen."

"I'm assuming that's because it's new," I declared. "I don't know, maybe you just missed this one."

I felt pretty smug. I was on the cutting edge of diet and fitness, thanks to Eliza.

But then I wasn't so sure when Dylan, sounding warier than ever, said, "Exactly what kinds of baby food are you supposed to eat on this so-called diet?"

Feeling less and less confident that Eliza's plan was legit, I softly replied, "I'm not doing that part of the plan, but I know for sure that pureed sweet potatoes are part of it."

"I don't know, Perry. Sounds sketchy, if you ask me."

Dylan was not only super fit, but he stayed up-to-date on just about every new diet trend and fitness craze out there. I had to admit it was odd he'd not heard of this one.

Quietly, he asked, "Who told you about this diet?"

What the hell, he already knew who I was secretly seeing.

"Eliza," I said.

He shot me a funny look. "You sure she's not just yanking your chain? You said she was mad that you couldn't remember that puck bunny you fucked. Maybe this is her idea of payback."

I thought about it, but concluded, "No, I don't think so. She told me about the diet before we ran into that chick at the club."

"Maybe she has a weird sense of humor, then?"

Again, I had to disagree. "No. She's a quirky girl, but not in that way. She's, like, super honest, man."

"We'll see."

He took out his phone and started googling.

"You that suspicious?"

"Yep."

Sighing, I conceded, "I probably should've done that right after she told me about the diet."

"No worries. I'm checking on it now."

After some clicking and scrolling, Dylan concluded, "Well, my friend, I have some bad news. There's not a single mention of a diet or fitness regimen, new or otherwise, where baby food or pacifiers are part of the program."

"Not one?"

"None."

"Shit."

This wasn't good. It meant one thing and one thing only—Eliza had lied.

Why would she do that?

I was so tied up about the prospect of Eliza playing me for a fool that I almost drove past Dylan's house.

"Whoa, man, I'm right there," he said, pointing to his home.

I dropped him off and turned around, ready to head to my own home.

By the time I pulled in my driveway, I was muttering to myself, "Google doesn't know everything."

Fuck, I hated this. I couldn't think straight. I couldn't imagine a single reason why Eliza would lie about the diet. On top of that, I was freaking exhausted from the trip. I clearly needed a nap.

"Yeah, after you get some sleep, you can figure it out," I assured myself.

Tired as I was, I ended up lingering downstairs for a few minutes. Only because I had a snack to eat.

Yeah, you guessed it—I'd gone ahead and picked up a donut on the way home from Dylan's. Those shops had been calling to me, man.

I spent the next several minutes savoring bites of chocolate-frosted goodness. After I was done, I sat there on the sofa, watching my fish dart around in the aquarium.

It appeared Eliza had taken good care of them the past few days. No casualties on her watch. Maybe she wasn't so mad at me, after all.

Then I remembered my conversation with Dylan and concluded *I* was a little pissed at *her*.

"I can't believe she lied about the diet," I murmured.

I couldn't deal with it now, though. I really needed some sleep.

I was so exhausted that I started discarding my clothes as I trudged up the stairs to my bedroom. By the time I reached my bedroom door, I was down to boxer briefs and nothing else.

I flipped on the light and… "*What the fuck?*"

There was a freaking puck bunny in my bed, naked as a jaybird from what I could see.

Wait, I knew this one—she was the girl from the club.

"Surprise, big boy!" she squealed.

Her tits jiggled as she tossed back the covers to reveal she was indeed completely nude.

"Come on to bed, Benny," she purred seductively. "Let Clarisse give you a proper welcome home."

TESTING, 1-2-3, TESTING, 1-2-3

ELIZA

The original test I'd come up with involved me hiding in Benny's bedroom closet so I could watch the action go down with my own two eyes.

Clarisse nixed that idea, claiming it'd be too weird.

As if entrapping Benny wasn't bizarre enough?

I was just happy she was actually going along with the plan so I agreed to wait out in the car.

After driving Clarisse to Benny's, I parked about a block away. It was a good spot, an empty lot where someone was building a house. There were a couple of parked construction trucks offering good cover, so I felt confident no one would notice me sitting there. Not that there were a lot of people milling around Benny's barely built-up neighborhood.

As I watched Clarisse disappear from view, I finally relaxed.

But minutes later when Benny's Porsche came barreling down the road, I tensed back up.

He was home.

Clarisse was in the house.

Game on.

"Please, God, let him pass this test," I murmured.

It had come down to this. Everything regarding where we'd go from here would be decided soon.

Clarisse was to make her move on Benny, as we planned, and text me his response.

This is crazy.

I had left the details of how to accomplish the seduction up to her. But I was having second thoughts. *Was that such a good idea?* Maybe I should've been more specific.

Oh, well. I could only hope Clarisse didn't take things too far. Benny was a man, after all, so I prayed she wouldn't make him an offer he absolutely could not refuse.

What began as a tiny ping of worry grew to outright panic when fifteen minutes passed and I'd still not received a text.

What if Benny failed the test?

Did I trust Clarisse to stop?

I wasn't so sure, and awful visions of Benny banging the hell out of her infiltrated my every thought.

I was up and out of that car in two minutes flat.

Racing down to the house, I was relieved to find the front door unlocked. Going in, I knew I might find Benny in a compromising position. What killed me was, if I did, I only had myself to blame.

"What the hell was I thinking?" I lamented to Clownie as I jogged past him.

He, of course, had no answer. Still, I totally imagined him yelling out, "Told you not to open a can of worms."

Worms, fish—oh, he was a funny little guy.

But what did he know?

I started upstairs, but soon faltered. "What the hell?"

There was a trail of discarded clothes—*Benny's* clothes—scattered the whole way up.

Ugh!

I couldn't stop now. I had to face whatever nightmare I'd made possible.

Blowing out a breath, I ascended to whatever hell lay before me. I was sure it was a horrific hell indeed when I reached the top of the stairs and heard voices down the hall. It was Benny and Clarisse.

I stopped to listen.

At least there was no grunting and groaning, just the murmur of normal talking. Still, I didn't like that this talking was occurring behind a closed door.

The voices continued as I approached. I didn't bother knocking when I got there, I just barged in.

Benny was standing off to the side, looking from me to Clarisse, who was *in* his freaking bed!

Focusing just on me, he exclaimed, "Eliza, what the ever-loving-fuck are you doing here?"

I opened my mouth to explain, feeling instantly bad for setting this up. That was when I noticed he had on nothing but boxers.

That explains the trail of clothes.

Fuming, I snapped, "Never mind why I'm here. What I'd like to know is why you're standing there in nothing but boxer briefs."

Before he could reply, I turned to Clarisse.

She was still lounging in his bed. And whoa, wait, where were *her* clothes? "Why are you naked, too?" I yelled at her.

"Oh, calm down," she admonished. "I had to go all in for this to work."

"And all in meant taking off all your clothes?" I screamed.

"Yes, it did. You said it was up to me to figure out how to get the job done. And I did what I had to do. Benny didn't take the bait, though." She looked disappointed—*bitch*! "So nothing happened."

I breathed the hugest sigh of relief, but reiterated, "Getting naked should *not* have been part of the test, Clarisse."

"You wanted it to be a test worth taking, right? You said you did."

"I did," I conceded.

Benny jumped in then. "Hey, what kind of test are we talking about here?"

Neither Clarisse nor I replied, and after a few seconds it was like it finally hit him that she and I were in on this together.

"How are you two friends, anyway?" he asked.

"We're not friends," Clarisse replied. "And this test thing was all her idea. She called me and asked for my help. I only agreed to be nice."

I coughed and sputtered. "Yeah, right, you agreed because I promised to introduce you to Dylan Culderway."

Benny, side-eyeing me, said, "What does he have to do with any of this?"

"Nothing, nothing at all," I assured him.

"Okay, but I still want to know what this test is all about, Eliza."

"It's a long story, Benny."

"One I'd like to hear."

Helpful—*not*—Clarisse jumped in then. "Your girlfriend was only trying to find out if you're a faithful guy, Benny. And good news—you are! For the record, Eliza"—she pinned me with an I-did-what-I-had-to look—"you didn't mention any specific rules on *how* to test him."

Oh, we were back to that.

Bristling, I snapped, "I was hoping you'd figure out a way to do it without having to take off *all* your damn clothes."

Benny threw up his hands. "Is anyone going to answer my question? What's this test you two keep referring to? I want the details."

I replied, "Okay, okay. I'll answer all your questions, I promise."

He crossed his arms over his wide, tatted chest, and when I faltered, he said, "I'm waiting."

Sighing, I confessed everything, at least, regarding the test.

"I needed to know if you still had a puck bunny problem, Benny. After that night at the club, I was just so torn. You didn't even remember you'd fucked Clarisse." She huffed in the background, and we both ignored her. "You have to realize, as a woman, I needed to know before I moved forward with a guy who's a player."

"Reformed player," he corrected.

"Okay, but still. I needed to know."

Softening, he said, "I passed, right?"

"You did."

"Does that mean we're back to being good, Eliza?"

His eyes met mine, and to my surprise, his emerald greens held forgiveness, not anger for me testing him. Even better, there was hope in those eyes, hope for *us*.

How could I say no to that?

"We're more than good, Benny," I proclaimed.

I wanted nothing more than to go to him, but there was still someone in the room. That someone cleared her throat, which made Benny, who also seemed to have forgotten she was there, frown.

He put up his hand. "Wait a minute."

"Hey," she snapped.

Ignoring her, he focused back on me, "I still have questions, Eliza."

"I'm sure you do."

"You're going to answer some of them right now."

"Um, okay."

"First," he began, "how did you know Clarisse's number?"

Uh-oh. "Um..."

How was I supposed to tell him I'd searched out his puck bunny directory?

Lucky for me—maybe—he figured it out.

"Shit, Eliza. You were at my house all alone."

I tried to joke, "There were fish here with me."

"Eliza..."

"Okay, okay. I was by myself. And, yes, I may have stumbled upon your directory."

Had I gone too far? Benny was an easygoing guy, but even he had his limits. It seemed he was letting it slide that I'd tested him. But was seeking out his puck bunny directory too much?

I was about to find out, till Clarisse butted in.

"Hey, what are y'all talking about? What directory? Like one with phone numbers? Do people still do that, write shit down like that? Or did you also raid Benny's cell phone, Eliza?"

The nerve!

"No, I didn't raid his cell phone," I said icily.

Turning back to Benny, I softly inquired, "Are you mad I looked for your directory? And are you pissed I got Clarisse in on this...test?" I sighed. "I went too far, I know, but I had to be sure I could trust you before...you know..." I waved my hand between us, and he raised a brow.

"You wanted to know I was done with other women before we got more serious."

"Yes." I peered at him sheepishly. "Can you forgive me?"

"Yes, I can forgive you for scoping out my directory."—*Phew!*—"But only if *you* can forgive *me* for having it in the first place."

"A directory with a rating system, no less," I reminded him.

"God, yes, that." He chuckled. "How embarrassing."

"More like"—I scowled—"how gross."

Giving me a chastising look, he said, "Like women don't ever rate men."

He had a point. "Okay, but still, Benny, *I* don't have a directory."

"Thank Christ for that."

Clarisse interjected, "So this directory, I'm in it, apparently. I'd like to know what kind of rating I got."

Benny looked away, smirking, but I couldn't resist.

With a fake smile, I sweetly replied, "You got four stars, honey."

"And that's out of five?"

Oh my God, this chick.

"Yes."

Clarisse preened. "Huh, that's a pretty good rating."

Benny couldn't even look at her, but I had to laugh. It was funny, now that he'd passed the test. I was happy he had. But more importantly, he'd forgiven me for testing him *and* for searching out his puck bunny directory.

I could only hope he'd be just as forgiving when he found out about Ava.

I was going to tell him real soon.

Just not today.

14

WORTH THE WAIT

BENNY

A fter Eliza left to drive Clarisse back to her car—but not before promising to return so we could talk some more—I thought about all that had occurred.

What she'd done was over the top, sure, but what I'd said was true. I wasn't mad about any of it. In a way, I was flattered. Eliza had not only searched out my directory, but she'd set up a crazy test to see what I'd do.

That meant she cared—a lot.

One thing I did wonder about was who had told Eliza about my directory in the first place. I sure hadn't said a word. The primary suspect was Lainey. She was Eliza's friend, and Nolan had probably mentioned it to her. It was too juicy not to. Plus, Nolan seemed not to want to see me with Eliza. Not for any bad reason, I was sure. My teammate was just looking out for me. He knew Coach T would throttle me into next year if he ever discovered I was messing around with his daughter.

Nolan need not worry, though. No one had to. My feelings for Eliza had grown from a lust-induced scheme to true interest. I wanted to build something with her, which still kind of blew me away.

Because of all my strong feelings for her, I ended up doing something I never thought I'd do, not in a million years.

When Eliza returned to the house, I suggested we do what Dylan had suggested—burn my once-beloved puck bunny directory.

"It'll be symbolic," I told her with a smile, echoing Dylan's words.

She looked wary. "Are you sure, Benny?"

I had to chuckle. She was trying to temper her tone to sound reasonable. Too bad it wasn't working. I could see the glee in her eyes at the idea of ridding the world of the puck bunny directory.

Yeah, she desperately wanted it gone.

No surprise there, seeing as she'd set up an elaborate ruse with one of the entries to test me. But here she was, willing to let me ultimately decide if we should burn the thing or not.

Good thing I'd already decided.

"I'm more than sure, babe." I offered her my hand. "Let's go get rid of it. That damn book is my last addiction, and it ends here."

Raising a brow, she asked, "What about donuts?"

"Ah, there are those. You got me there."

She squeezed my hand. "I think I can live with that one, Benny. If you can, that is."

"Are you kidding? I'm never giving up donuts."

"Then don't," she said.

Yep, this was definitely the girl for me.

The donuts made me think about the pacifier and my conversation with Dylan. I thought about questioning Eliza, but when she left the room to go pee and I saw the pink pacifier in her open purse, I figured she'd probably made up the diet on her own. That's why Dylan couldn't find it with Google. Oh well, whatever works, right?

She returned, and hand-in-hand, we went downstairs.

We stood in front of the massive stone fire pit out back and watched the directory burn to a crisp. As the pages turned black, then gray, then to ash, I felt no regret. Why would I? I had finally turned a corner.

I think Eliza realized that, too.

That's why what happened next was only natural.

Turning to me, bathed in the glow from the flames, Eliza slid her arms up around my neck. She murmured a loving, "Benny..."

"Yes?"

Standing on her tiptoes, she pressed her lips to mine. "I think it's time we make a little heat of our own."

I could not agree more.

I was still wearing only boxer briefs, and Eliza had on nothing but a thin tee and short shorts. But fuck, it felt like it was getting hotter and hotter by the fire.

"I think you're right," I replied.

I kissed her then, all softly and sweetly. But when I felt her body respond, my tongue plunged into her mouth. Though it felt somewhat frenzied, it was different. Better than the first time we'd messed around. That had been pure lust and fun.

This was...more.

Gathering her up in my arms, my heart swelled with a joy I'd never known. I carried her inside the house and up to my bedroom. As I laid her back on my bed, I peeled away her shorts, her tee, and her bra. But before she'd allow me to slide her lacy panties down her legs, she made me grab a condom.

"I'm on birth control," she said, "but extra protection is always a good idea."

After paging through the now-destroyed PB directory, I figured she was worried I harbored some gross disease.

I was good, though, and quickly informed her, "I'm clean, Eliza. If that's what you're really worried about."

I kind of wanted to feel all of her, which I hadn't done with a woman in years.

"We get tested all the time," I went on. "And I *always* wrap up my junk."

"It's not that," she insisted, her hand moving to caress the rough stubble on my cheek. "It's just that birth control can fail sometimes."

Her insistence made me curious if there was more to what she was saying. Maybe she'd had a pregnancy scare and that's why she was unwilling to budge on the issue. I respected her wishes no matter what, so I dropped the subject and retrieved a condom from a pack I kept by the bed.

With the interruption and ensuing discussion, the mood was waning.

Rolling back to face her, I said, "Let's start over, okay?"

She nodded. "That sounds good to me."

I began touching her then, and letting her know, "I want this to be perfect for you, Eliza."

"I want that for you, as well."

I told her the truth. "It already is."

"So let's make it better." Wrapping her leg around my waist, she ground herself into me. I knew what she wanted, so I shifted until my heavy cock was pressed up to her pussy.

Her panties were still on, and man, were they soaked.

She rocked along my length, murmuring shit like, "Make me feel good, Benny. Please, I need you to."

"I need you, too, and I plan to," I assured her, ridding her of her panties, at last.

Good thing she wanted the condom on me. Otherwise, I might've lost it right there and slid into her. Waiting was better, however. It gave me an opportunity to make sure she came before we were one.

After she had fallen apart twice, I finally slipped on a condom.

She was so hot and bothered that she lined up our bodies and begged, "Benny, please, please, I need you now. Don't keep me waiting a minute longer."

I plunged into her, engulfed and overwhelmed by her warmth. I thought I might explode right then, condom or not.

I even had to stop for a minute and hold still, which made her ask, "Is something wrong?"

"Are you kidding? Everything is perfect, Eliza."

"It is," she agreed, her eyes meeting mine.

"I want you so much," I rasped, overcome with emotion.

"You have me, Benny. You have me right here."

I did. But what she didn't know was how much *she* had *me*.

And hell if that didn't feel just right.

15

WHAT CAN I SAY?

ELIZA

The first time with Benny... What can I say?

It was sweeter than I thought it would be.

It was better than expected.

What about hot?

Yes. Hell, yes.

Still, it was more than all those things. I can honestly say I fell a little harder after we were together.

No, wait. I fell a lot harder.

Why did it work that way for women? Hormones, maybe? Or were our hearts too open to begin with?

I wasn't sure either way. I just knew I'd also fallen hard for Ava's father after the first time we were together, too.

But this felt completely different.

Ava's father hadn't cared about me in any way. I was just a fun lay to him. Benny had true feelings for me. Of that, I had no doubt. I mean, the dude burned his pussy directory for me. That said a lot.

There was one problem still on the horizon—me. I felt like the world's biggest bitch for continuing to keep Ava from him.

I was still committed to telling him, but now that the time was upon me I was scared. What if he couldn't find it in his heart to forgive me?

I could maybe convince him it was a lie by omission, and that might soften the blow.

No, there was just no good way to do it. I needed to simply sit him down and pour my heart out.

And then hope he understood.

I was ready, I was prepared.

I even had my phone in my hand, set to call Benny so we could choose a time to meet and talk.

But then something happened—I received a rare communication from Ava's father.

And that changed everything.

It'd been so long since I'd last heard from him that I'd kind of forgotten he was the big reason for me keeping Ava a secret in the first place. What with all his to-do about keeping his identity from getting out.

I didn't even like to *say* his stupid name. But I did when it flashed across my phone screen, indicating he was calling.

"Drew Chidders," I practically spat. "What the hell could he possibly want?"

Drew Chidders was an up-and-coming forward with the Dallas Stars. He also happened to be Ava's absentee dad.

And now he was calling me, right when I was about to call Benny.

I stared down at the phone, watching as my own little personal code name for Drew—*Dickhead*—flashed on the screen again.

He lived up to that moniker so well, and I felt sure he would today.

I should've ignored him, but I didn't. I answered just in case he was calling about his daughter. Maybe he was finally ready to step up to the plate and be a dad to her.

Nope.

Dickhead wasn't reaching out to ask about his sweet little girl.

There was no "how's she doing, Eliza."

Nor an "I'd love to finally meet her."

Instead, he'd called to make certain I was still keeping his identity a secret.

"Of course I'm still keeping your identity a secret," I snapped, feeling instantly annoyed, as it messed with my plan to tell Benny about Ava.

"Good," he replied, unfazed by my tone. "I'm only checking because we're playing the Wolves week after next."

"Yes, I know. I saw it on the schedule."

"I can't stress enough that I don't want any trouble at that game, Eliza."

"What the hell does that mean?" I questioned, bristling.

"It means don't even *think* about pulling any of that girly I-need-attention bullshit."

I'd been aggressive in pursuing Drew, especially after we'd originally hooked up. But I'd grown a lot since then. He was the last man I'd ever want attention from now.

"I'm no longer the girl you once knew," I informed the jerk.

"Good."

I still wasn't sure what he expected me to do at the upcoming game. What would be so awful?

"What exactly are you worried I'll do?" I asked.

Guffawing, like I was some kind of a big joke, he said, "With you, Eliza, who knows? You can be fucking crazy."

"Fuck you, Drew."

"You better check that attitude, bitch."

"Suck my clit, Drew."

"Been there, done that."

I hated him, I really did.

Finally mad, he snapped, "I don't want you pulling some stunt at the game, drawing attention to yourself to distract me."

He was so full of himself.

"How would I do that?" I asked, curious and not having any idea what his nutty imagination was conjuring up.

"For one, I could see you sitting in the front row with that baby in your arms. And, Eliza, I don't need a distraction like that during what's sure to be a big game for me."

Oh my God, this guy.

I yelled into the phone, "For the record, your baby is not a distraction, asshole!"

"Oh, that's nice."

Suddenly overwhelmed with emotion—hurt, anger, disbelief—I whispered, "Shut up, Drew. Just, please, shut up."

Did he?

No.

"For your information, I'm on track to surpass the number of goals I had this time last season. And *that* is my only concern at the moment."

"Clearly," I choked out.

With my heart lodged in my throat, I had no more words for this man. I couldn't believe he'd behave so callously, say the things he said. I didn't care about my own stupid self—I was done with the prick—but Ava… God, Ava. I'd given her such a shitty father.

"Eliza, did you hear me?" he droned on. "Making sure you and I are on the same page is why I called."

On the same page? He and I?

Ha. There was no he and I. And as for pages, we weren't even in the same book.

Out of all the emotions I was grappling with, anger finally won out. And I lost it.

"Who the hell do you think you are, Drew? There is no same page, and there is no you and I. *You* walked away, so *you* don't get a say in anything."

Smugly, he retorted, "Is that so?"

"Yes, it is so."

Chuckling, he said, "Do I need to remind you of the money I deposit in your account every month for Ava's care? Those are some pretty big sums, Eliza."

"You can't buy me into behaving the way you want me to, Drew."

"Sure I can."

Icily, I replied, "Well, then, *I* can take *you* to court and ask for more money. I'd get it, too. So maybe that's what I should do."

I didn't care about the money; I was tired of him and his power plays. Plus, I'd finally grown a backbone these past few months.

But then he stopped me in my take-that-asshole tracks when he coldly replied, "You do that and I'll fight you for custody of my child."

"Oh, *now* she's your child? How convenient."

Softly, and in a tone that frankly scared the hell out of me, he said,

"I mean it. Don't fight me on this, Eliza. And don't be a smartass. I have more money and better access to attorneys than you do. I can make you look like an unfit slut of a mother in an instant. Plus, I'm not above telling the court that you keep me from my child."

"But that's a lie," I whispered, stunned that he'd even stoop to this level. "You *never* ask to see her."

"They don't know that. I'll do whatever it takes. I'll win at any cost."

"You will, won't you?"

"You bet your ass I will."

He'd broken me again, this time with his words. The first had been him not wanting to acknowledge his daughter.

Overwhelmed and feeling small, I started to cry. This prick had me by the ovaries.

I wanted to reach through the phone and punch him in the head.

I wanted to scream and rant.

But the only thing I could do was call him the hell out.

Summoning strength for Ava's sake, I hissed, "How dare you threaten to take Ava away from me. You never wanted her, you've said so yourself again and again. You never even call to ask about her. Never, Drew. Not once have you contacted me about her. It's always all about you. You don't care about her *at all*. Yet you dare to threaten m—"

"Settle down, Eliza. I'm not going to do anything if we can work this out. I'm simply reminding you of what's at stake. I consistently pay what we agreed upon. And I leave you two alone. So now I'm only asking for you to keep that baby away from the game. *And* for you to continue to keep the fact that I'm her father a secret. If you can do those two simple things, I won't come after you."

"You make me sick," I murmured.

I'd never planned to take Ava to the game he was referring to, but this threw a wrench in my plans to tell Benny about her. He'd surely ask who the dad was, right? Maybe he wouldn't, but if he did, what would I say?

"So we have an agreement?" he prompted when I remained quiet.

Before I agreed to anything he was going to hear about his daughter, whether he wanted to or not. It was the least he could do.

"Ava's doing great, by the way," I began, still choked up but determined. "She rolls over on her own now. And she smiles *so* much, especially when she hears music. She's a happy little baby. She's bright and alert and just the sweetest—"

He cut me off. Cut me off so he didn't have to hear about the child he'd help create. I didn't listen to half of what he said next, but the bits and pieces that came through sounded like more bullshit about him and his career milestones.

Blah, blah, blah...

I finally agreed to his stupid terms, and he let me go. But I couldn't stop shaking. Drew had rattled me. Just knowing what he could do to me and Ava, like split us apart, scared the living crap out of me.

I'd never needed a friend to talk to more than I did in that moment.

So I called Lainey.

I didn't know what I was going to say, but with the way I was feeling I probably would've confessed the whole sordid tale to her, Drew be damned.

Good thing I got her voice mail. I remembered then that she was out of town for an interview.

"Shit," I murmured as I disconnected.

If I'd gotten to Benny before Drew had called, he'd already know about Ava. Then I could've called him and told him what had just happened. He'd probably volunteer to kick the shit out of Drew.

That made me smile, especially since Benny would have the perfect opportunity to kick his ass legitimately—on the ice at the upcoming Wolves-Stars game.

I couldn't involve him, though. Not now. I sincerely feared what Drew would do if I told his secret to, of all people, a fellow professional hockey player. If Dickhead found out, he'd wreak all sorts of havoc in my and Ava's lives, just like he promised.

I certainly didn't want him cutting off payments or, God forbid, fighting for custody. He obviously had no interest in his daughter, and I knew in my heart that if he ever had her full time, he'd just pass her off to a nanny. It scared me to think of how horrible Ava's life would become if that jackass ever got custody of her.

One thing was made abundantly clear that day—I was pretty much fucked.

I feared sharing Ava's existence with Benny.

And I feared not sharing it with him.

There was no good outcome to any of this.

Suddenly needing to see my baby more than anything else in the universe, I went into her nursery and picked her up.

"I love you so much," I whispered to her as I held her close to my heart.

It was up to me and me alone to make sure Ava grew up feeling loved and treasured. Her father wasn't going to provide any of that.

I had a sense that someone else might, though. Despite his past faults, I knew in my heart that Benny would make a great stepfather. He carried a lot of genuine goodness in his heart.

Too bad it was a silly fantasy to even entertain that he'd have a chance to be a father to Ava. That could never happen now. Drew had made sure of it.

I rocked Ava in my arms and began to cry.

With tears streaming down my cheeks, I told her about the call. I apologized over and over for Drew being her father.

She, of course, had no idea what I was going on about. She just looked up at me and cooed.

And that just made me cry even harder.

16

SAMSON HAS NOTHING ON ME

BENNY

Graham called early the next week to see if I wanted to grab lunch.

"Friday good for you?" he asked.

"Yep," I replied.

I hadn't attended a meeting in a couple of weeks. I presumed this was his roundabout way of checking in on me.

Good thing I was doing great.

There was no drinking, no illegal substances, and certainly no random women. I couldn't wait to tell him how only life itself had me flying high these days, thanks to Eliza.

I was just so damn into that girl.

I also planned to share with him my new status as a guy in a committed relationship. Graham was sure to be happy I'd found such an amazing woman, one who was fine with knowing every detail of my sordid past and still willing to accept me for, well, me.

How amazing was that?

I was so up and ready for Friday's lunch that I arrived way too early. With an hour to spare, I sat in my parked car and opened an app to see what was of interest in the area.

What intrigued me immediately was seeing there was a barbershop only a block away.

That's where I need to go.

The recent positive changes in my life called for something monumental. I'd already been itching to do something to commemorate how far I'd come. I was considering a new tattoo, but something seemed more fitting now—I'd shed my wild past by shedding my wild hair.

I hopped out of my car and practically ran down to the barbershop. I was that excited and ready to have my long blond locks lopped off.

"Give me a buzz cut," I told the kindly old barber the second I was seated in his chair.

"You sure you want to do that, young man?" he asked, peering at me uneasily from the reflection in the mirror on the wall.

Ah, crap, he knew who I was. That explained his reticence.

There were fans, and quite a few of them at that, who believed my strength on the ice came from my long hair. Not unlike Samson in that old biblical tale.

"Dude…" My eyes met his as I shook my head and laughed. "It's all good, I promise."

"I don't know," he hedged. "I don't want to be the reason why the Wolves's season tanks."

I assured him nothing like that would happen.

"We have a good team, man. And I'm having a great season. Shorter hair won't affect my play. If anything, it'll make me more aerodynamic."

That last was bullshit, but he seemed to buy it.

"Okay, if you're absolutely certain, I'll do it."

I handed him the scissors. "Go for it," I urged.

There was no backing out now.

Over the next thirty minutes, I chilled in the barbershop chair, watching swaths of blond hair rain down onto the floor. When the old barber finished cutting, he brought out an electric shaver and buzzed down what little bit was left close to my head.

When it was all over, I felt cool and bare. And I liked it.

Peering at my reflection, I ran a hand over my stubbly scalp. There was some scruff on my face that matched, and I thought it went well with the closely shorn look.

"I like it," I told the barber, nodding approvingly.

He blew out a breath, relieved.

"Good luck the rest of the season," he said as I stood.

"Thanks, man."

I tried to pay for the cut, but he was having none of it. "This one's on the house," he said.

I was sure to give him a huge tip to make up for the free cut.

As I was leaving, I told him my next goal would be for him.

"There'll be no team slump just because you cut my hair."

"I hope not," he said.

"There won't be," I murmured before I left the barbershop.

As I started down to the restaurant, I felt the need to assure myself, "Superstitions are silly."

I didn't really believe that, not after what had happened when I'd joked about touching Brent's sticks.

"Yeah, we lost the game that night. Shit."

I hoped like hell my strength didn't really lie in my hair, or we were all fucked.

To appease all the gods—hockey or otherwise—when I came upon a ladder where workers were changing a lightbulb at a strorefront, I made sure *not* to walk under it.

It couldn't hurt, right?

I was really starting to stress, so when I stepped into the restaurant and saw Graham was already there, I let out a giant relieved breath. I was ready to talk about anything to get my mind off jinxes and superstitions.

It took a minute for Graham to recognize me.

Finally, wide-eyed, he said, "Whoa, what the hell happened to your hair, Perry?"

With a huge grin on my face—I'd managed to shock the usually unflappable Graham—I replied, "It's gone, man."

"I can see that. But what prompted such a major change?"

The hostess arrived then, so my explanation had to wait. But once we were seated, I tried to provide Graham with a solid reason.

"About this change…" I gestured to my head. "A lot has happened lately. I felt like it was time to let go of the past in some symbolic way."

"So there went the hair, huh?" Graham replied.

"Yep."

Looking suddenly concerned, he asked, "Everything's okay, though, right?"

I nodded. "Yeah, yeah, things are better than ever."

I filled him in then, getting him up to speed on all things Eliza. I'd gotten to the part that she was different from any other woman I'd known when our lunch entrees arrived.

"Bottom line is that I really care about her," I stated proudly as I picked up my burger.

He leaned back. "Wow, I can tell."

"She's just so genuine," I continued after taking a bite. "She's simple, but in a totally good way."

"Tell me more," he said.

"Well, Eliza is cute…and sexy…and crazy fun. But the best part is she's got to be the most honest, down-to-earth person I've ever met."

Softly, he said, "This Eliza sounds like someone really special."

"She is, man. She's the kind of woman you hold onto, that's for sure. You're going to like her, Graham. She makes me want to keep moving forward in really positive ways."

He canted his head to the left, a signature Graham move. "How so, Benny?"

"For one thing—and you're gonna love this one—she got me to get rid of my directory."

He dropped his fork into the giant salad he was eating. "No way."

"See," I laughed. "I knew I'd get you with that one. But, yeah, we actually burned it together. It's nothing but a pile of ash out in the fire pit at the back of my house."

Graham shook his head. "It's hard to believe, Benny."

"Believe it, man. My days of nailing puck bunnies are finished."

"Shit. This girl really *is* something special," Graham marveled.

"She's the kind of girl you fall in love with," I murmured, not even thinking when I said it.

That was okay. Maybe it was how I needed to recognize the truth. What I'd blurted out was me being honest—I could really see myself falling in love with Eliza.

In fact, I was pretty much already there.

Graham saw the look on my face, and smiling, he held up his water glass and said, "Congratulations, Benny."

I had only two words to say back to him, "Thanks, man."

17

SECRETS DEEPEN

ELIZA

Benny and I started spending a ton of time together. And every minute of it was nothing short of spectacular. Well, *mostly* every minute of it was good. The first few days after he'd gotten his hair cut were a little rocky.

That was all my fault. Still reeling from my phone conversation with Drew, I was freaked out by Benny's haircut. It made me question why he'd done such a thing out of the blue.

Was it for some negative reason I'd yet to discover?

Damn Drew. He's making me paranoid.

The night after Benny did the deed, we met out for a late-night dinner date. I didn't know yet what he'd done.

Needless to say, when he walked into the diner, I sat there in the booth I'd procured for us earlier, staring at him in shock.

"Oh my God," I blurted out when he sat down across from me. "You chopped off all your beautiful hair!"

"Aw, crap." He ran his hand over his nearly bald head. "You hate it, don't you?"

"No, I don't," I admitted, composing myself.

Grudgingly, I admitted, "It actually suits you really well, gives you a sexy kind of vibe."

It was true, and he said, "Thanks, babe."

The closely cropped hair combined with the tiny bit of stubble he was sporting made him look rugged and just so freaking *male*. Several women had turned around to look at him, all with appreciation in their eyes. Not because he was Benjamin Perry, hockey player extraordinaire, but because this new version of him was positively scorching.

Even much younger women were enamored, as evidenced when a girl of about sixteen approached our booth and asked if she could take a quick selfie with Benny.

"You're really rocking your new look, Mr. Perry," she said.

"Thanks. But could a picture wait till after dinner?" Benny gestured to the menus we'd not yet looked at. "If you don't mind holding off for about an hour, I'll let you take as many pics as you want."

Looking dejected, she replied, "I would wait, but I'm here with my parents. We already ate and they're gonna want to leave any minute."

She peered down at the #29 Wolves jersey she was wearing. It was Benny's number.

"Maybe I'll just run into you some other time," she mumbled.

Benny glanced over at me. "Would you mind?" he mouthed.

I didn't mind. The girl was sweet, young, and unthreatening, so I whispered, "Of course not."

The girl heard my assent and started bouncing up and down on her Chuck-clad toes. "Oh my God, you guys are so nice. Thank you so much!"

Benny slid out of the booth to stand next to the girl for the photo. She leaned in to him, smiling, her smartphone held high in the air.

It was cute. She was so tiny that Benny had to scrunch down to fit in the frame.

The girl snapped her pic, and then motioned for me to join them for the next one.

"You should be in this one," she said. "You're Mr. Perry's girlfriend, right?"

Though we'd never officially declared our status, mostly because we were still keeping the fact that we were even dating under wraps, I assumed we were indeed a couple.

Nonetheless, it was wonderful to hear Benny reply, "She sure is."

Feeling giddy, I slid out of the booth and stepped over to be in the picture with him and the girl.

I spared not a second thought about it. I don't think he did either. The pic was snapped, and the girl thanked us, and then she left.

The dinner seemed to go by quickly after that, too fast to really "talk."

By the time Benny and I returned to his house for some *Netflix and chill*, I was back to ruminating on the motivation for his haircut.

I decided right away that the "chill" part was going to have to wait. I needed to know if his action had been a response to something bad before any sexing got started.

"Let's watch something first," I said as he hovered over me, ready to kiss me, on the sofa.

He pulled back. "Why? Is something wrong?"

"No." I was unsure how to jump into what was worrying me, so I added, "I just feel like relaxing for a bit."

"Okay, babe."

He sat back and turned on the TV, and I snuggled into the corner of the sofa. I tried to get into the movie he selected, but just couldn't.

"You want to pick something else?" he said ten minutes in.

He must've noticed my lack of laughter, even at the funny parts.

"No," I replied.

Benny stretched out on the sofa and rested his head in my lap. "You sure?"

"Yes." I placed my hand on his buzzed hair. "It just feels so different now," I murmured.

He glanced up at me. "I know, right? It really does."

"Do you like it?"

"I do. It's way cooler."

"I bet."

We resumed watching the movie. Well, Benny did. I was busy gearing up to get to the bottom of this big change he'd made.

"You know," I began, clearing my throat, "it's kind of a major thing when someone has hair as long as yours...and they get it all chopped off on a whim."

Benny hit *Pause* and rolled onto his back. Peering up at me, he frowned. I could tell he was worried.

"You really don't like it, do you?" He smiled sadly. "You were just saying nice things at the restaurant to make me feel good."

"No, no, that's not true. I do like it, Benny. You look super-hot. I'm just worried about the motivation behind the cut."

He sat up. "Ah, you want to know why I did it, eh?"

"Yeah, Benny, I kind of do."

"Well, first you need to believe there was nothing negative behind it. I promise you that. In fact, I got it all chopped off for a really good reason."

"You did?"

"Yes." He looked over at me. "I wanted to do something major to mark that I'm finally letting go of the past. Like, in every freaking way imaginable."

I knew he was referring to the directory we'd burned, so I said, "That makes sense."

He smiled, and wow, he really was stunning. Long hair, short hair, no hair—he was a god.

"It's not permanent, you know?" he said. "It'll grow back."

I sat up next to him. Shit, I'd come off as too negative. I hadn't intended to, and he needed to know that.

"I just wanted to make sure it wasn't a kneejerk reaction to something bad, Benny."

"Something bad?" He raised a brow. "What could possibly be bad? My life is finally on track in every way."

Though he left it at that, his eyes seemed to question if there was something more with *me*, something he didn't know that he should.

Was there ever!

I couldn't tell him about Ava. Not after the conversation with Drew.

"No, there's nothing bad," I said, laughing nervously. "Why would there be? I was just worrying over nothing."

"You shouldn't worry so much, sweetheart."

Ha, from his lips to God's ears!

I wanted to assure him we were good, so I said, "I think it's wonderful you chose to make a symbolic gesture to celebrate all you've overcome. You should be proud of yourself, Benny."

I meant what I said, but I kept thinking, *If only I could say the same for my own self.*

"Come here, Eliza."

Benny pulled me to him and wrapped me up in his big bear arms.

I felt instantly comforted.

Swallowed up by Benny Perry made for a very comfortable place, like a cocoon of security and warmth.

Too bad I'd probably end up losing him.

18

UNRAVELING

BENNY

I f there was one dude I couldn't stand, it was this forward, this fucking right winger for the Dallas Stars, named Drew Chidders.

Fuck.

Even his name sounded asshole-ish. But man, did it ever fit him.

Drew was a major prick, a full-of-himself kind of guy. He was a dirty player to boot. We'd never gotten along, not on the ice or off.

I'd have to deal with him soon enough, though. We had a game against the Stars that was starting in a few short hours.

I couldn't believe we were well into December already. Nearly three months into the season and the Wolves were flying high. We kept moving from second place to first, then back again, in the division standings. It just depended on who was hot, us or the team we were neck and neck with—the Dallas Stars.

Despite all my worrying about superstitions, my haircut hadn't affected my play in any negative way. I was playing magnificently. Other things were great, as well—like me and Eliza.

Only thing I didn't like was that we were still sneaking around. No one knew about me and her, except for Dylan and Graham.

But I soon discovered we weren't the only ones keeping things on the down-low.

Nolan shocked the shit out of everyone when he up and married Lainey Shelburne. No one even knew they were officially dating. Well, I knew. But I always thought it was too volatile to last.

Was I ever wrong.

I had to laugh at how they reminded me of Eliza and me. To keep up our own farce, she and I had to pretend like we barely knew each other at their impromptu wedding, and at the reception afterward.

That kind of sucked. I couldn't dance with her, or love up on her the way I would've liked. I didn't give a shit anymore if the whole world knew we were together, and neither did she. But there was one thing holding us back—not knowing how her father would react when he found out about us.

If her dad hadn't been my coach, it wouldn't have mattered. But he was, and I was already far from one of his favorite players. Keeping our relationship from him was the only option for the time being.

Too bad Eliza and I had forgotten about the selfie the girl at the restaurant had taken. It was the one thing that had the power to reveal us to the world, the impetus that could unravel everything.

And that's exactly what happened.

It started during the game with the Dallas Stars and just spiraled downward after that. The unraveling technically began *before* the game even started. I just didn't realize it till later. I should've wondered, though, when a couple of the rookie guys on our team started passing around their phones and snickering like crazy.

It was weird, but I paid them no heed.

My mistake.

When the game got underway, I forgot all about rookies and their phones. I became preoccupied with the battle that was going in between me and fucking Drew Chidders.

Our hatred for one another had reignited as soon as we hit the ice. And then, early in the first period, as I was heading into a corner to retrieve the puck, Drew came out of freaking nowhere and barreled into me.

It was a good solid check, not boarding. I was even about to give him props for it. But then the prick turned around and sneered at me.

"You are one shady motherfucker, like *literally*," he said.

Huh?

We started battling for the puck, and I snapped at him, "What the fuck are you talking about, Chidders?"

"Like you don't know—"

That was all I heard because I'd come up with the puck and had skated away.

Brent was in front of the goal, covered by two Stars's defenders. But then I saw an opportunity. With the goaltender focused on the players in front of the net, a sliver of space had opened up on the far side.

I took full advantage of it, burying the puck in an instant.

He shoots and scores!

The home crowd went nuts, and after celebrating with my teammates, I looked up into the crowd. I was hoping to find Eliza, but she wasn't in her usual spot. I checked again a couple minutes later, figuring she'd gone to get nachos or something. But now there was actually someone else in her seat. They'd been the one running out for nachos.

It was weird. I mean, Eliza rarely missed a game. I guessed since it was finals week she'd decided to stay home and study.

Yeah, that had to be it.

We were up by one goal for a while, but then that fucker Chidders scored late in the second. He only got the goal because one of the Stars's goons had slashed Nolan across the wrist, taking him out of play.

Nolan left the ice injured and didn't return for the third. That had me a little concerned, but I had no time to dwell on it. Chidders was all over me again, even going so far as to hook me at one point.

The referee was right there and called the penalty.

"Fucking moron," I murmured as Drew skated past me on his way to the penalty box to serve his time.

He heard me and slowed to a stop.

"Laugh now, Perry," he said. "I'll have my turn when your coach figures out you're fucking his daughter."

Wait, how could he know that?

"What the fuck are you yammering on about?" I barked. "How could you even know such a thing?"

"Wouldn't you like to know, fuckface."

"Yeah, I kind of would."

We started circling each other, until the linesmen skated over to make sure we didn't start fighting.

"What I wouldn't do to be present when *that* conversation goes down," Drew yelled back over his shoulder as he was ushered away.

I was stumped. How the fuck could he have found out about us? It was truly a mystery. I couldn't imagine how that asshole could know I was with Eliza when no one else did.

Or, shit, did they?

I looked around, and for this one long minute I felt like everyone's eyes were on me.

Brent snapped me out of it when he skated by and tapped me with his stick.

"Are you all right, Benny?"

"Yeah." I shook my head, casting off my crazy thoughts. "I'm fine."

I wasn't, though. I could barely concentrate the rest of the game. As a result, I made some key mistakes, and Coach T benched me for the remainder of the third. That was really saying something since we were down a player already with Nolan out with the injured wrist.

"Get your head together," Coach barked at me as time ticked down. "I don't want to lose you, too."

Hmm, he didn't seem *too* angry with me. That meant he didn't know about me and Eliza, at least not yet. I was still trying to figure out how Chidders knew.

Fuck, I hope it doesn't have anything to do with why some of the rookie players were huddled around their phones before the game.

One thing for sure, I needed to find out.

Back in the locker room, I was all set to confront the young guys to see what had been so amusing. First, though, I wanted to shower and dress. I did so in record time, but before I could get to the rookies, Coach raced into the locker room and pulled me aside.

Looking angrier than I'd ever seen him, he ground out, "I need to talk with you immediately, Perry."

I nodded. "Okay."

I had a bad feeling he now knew what Chidders had known. And because of that, I followed him to what I suspected would be my doom.

19

SELFIE SHOWDOWN

ELIZA

Due to that awful discussion with Drew, I decided to skip the Stars-Wolves game altogether when it came around.

I'd never planned to take Ava, like Drew thought I had, but now I also had no desire to subject myself to watching her jackass father on the ice.

I made no mention of the game one way or the other to Benny in the days leading up to it. Though I was sure he assumed I'd be there.

I hoped he might not notice my absence, but if he did and asked I had a valid excuse—there was too much studying to do. It wasn't a lie since we were in the middle of winter finals week.

I didn't bother to watch the game on TV, for the same reason I didn't go to it. I wanted no part of Drew. I even went so far as to silence my phone so I wouldn't receive alerts.

I planned to study hard and already had several books spread across my bed in preparation. Ava was asleep in the next room, and the baby monitor was on. So far, things had been quiet. She'd been sleeping a lot more soundly lately. Once she was down, she was out.

As a result, I was über productive that night. By ten o'clock, I felt more than prepared for the upcoming exams.

"I should probably get some sleep now," I murmured to myself as I picked up my phone for the first time in hours.

I was readying to set the alarm for the morning when I noticed I had dozens of texts and voice mails. I wasn't sure yet about the voice mails, but the texts were all from Lainey.

Although none of them made any sense when I scrolled through them.

Did you see the picture yet, Eliza?

What's going on?

Are you and Benny dating?

Crap, I'm glad for you if you are. I mean, you look really happy in the picture. What about your dad, though?

What picture?

And how did she know about me and Benny?

Even more concerning was what did my dad know?

I was about to find out.

When I checked voice mail, there were three messages, all from my father. He wanted me to come to the arena to meet him at his office—immediately.

"We need to talk," he somberly stated in one foreboding message.

Shit. I was in for it. And I didn't dare consider what was in store for poor Benny. I doubted it was an invite to our next family dinner based on the latest text from Lainey—the one that had the picture in question attached.

More texts came in, and it seemed everyone knew about me and Benny. Everyone in my life, including my father, had seen the picture. The damn selfie the girl at the restaurant had taken—the one of me, her, and Benny—had been released to the world. I didn't care about the general population. It was the hockey world that concerned me, specifically my dad.

Crap, our secret was out.

All anyone had to do was look at the photo, which in and of itself was kind of cute. But with the way Benny was staring down at me, no one could miss the look of utter adoration on his face. I was returning that look, making it obvious we were way into each other.

But the proof that left no doubt was the girl had captioned the photo—*me with Benjamin Perry and His Pretty Girlfriend.*

Yep, my dad was going to kill me.

And probably string up Benny by his balls.

Drastic times called for drastic measures. I knew of only one person who could calm my dad and make him see reason—a tiny little girl who, with one smile, could melt anyone's heart.

20

WHAT AM I MISSING

BENNY

"Have a seat, Benjamin." Coach T gestured for me to take the chair across from him.

We were in his office, and I sat down resignedly.

Fuck.

Coach looked like the man with the power, sitting behind his desk all stern-like. Still, I couldn't imagine what I'd done to warrant a trip, an escorted one at that, to his office.

Was he pissed about the way I'd flaked out at the end of the game? Could that have been enough to make him this irate?

If so, I better fix it...and fast.

"Look, Coach," I began, "if this is about my play at the end of the third, I assure you that was a one-time—"

"This is not about the fucking game," he growled.

Coach Townsend wasn't usually a growler, so to say I was taken aback would've been an understatement.

"Okaaay," I drawled.

He tossed his phone over to me then, and I caught it with ease. "What's this?" I asked.

"It's a phone," he deadpanned. "I suggest you take a look at what's on the screen."

I peered down...and shit—there was the selfie the girl at the restaurant had taken.

My first reaction was, *wow, what a great picture!*

Good thing I didn't say that out loud.

"Umm," I murmured instead.

Through clenched teeth, Coach T said, "There had better be a good explanation for this."

I made a decision not to make things worse by lying. I'd been ready for a while to tell the world, which included Coach T, about my relationship with Eliza.

"Sir," I began, easing into it, "I don't really have one."

"That's hardly an explanation, Perry."

"I don't know what you want me to say."

I could feel anger roiling off him. Good thing there was a desk between us.

"For starters," he ground out, "why don't you tell me why this photo would seem to indicate from the caption that *my* daughter is *your* girlfriend?"

Now was the time. But it wasn't easy. Still, if you're going down with the ship, you may as well revel in the drowning.

At last, I replied, "Sir, the caption isn't a lie. Eliza is my girlfriend."

Ah, it felt good to tell the truth.

But Coach didn't share my relief. He actually looked kind of... smug?

Leaning back in his chair, like he knew something I didn't, he said, "She is, now is she? And just how well do you think you know Eliza, Mr. Perry?"

Tread carefully, tread carefully. He's calling you Mr. Perry now. That's worse than Benjamin.

"Uh, I'd say pretty well, sir."

"So how come I've never seen you at our house?"

"I've been there," I shot back, defensive. "But," I conceded, "only one time."

"Uh-huh, I see."

He looked all-knowing and even surer of himself. It was like something had just been confirmed for him.

What the hell could it be?

If he expected me to just go away, he was sadly mistaken.

Clearing my throat, I said, "Sir, I have to tell you that though it was wrong to hide our relationship from you, it doesn't mean it's not the real deal. I care for Eliza. In fact, I think I'm in love with her."

Wow, did I just say that out loud?

Yep, I had.

I meant it, though. There was no doubt anymore that I definitely loved Eliza. Forget falling—I was already there.

Coach shook his head, like he felt bad for me.

What? "What the hell is going on?" I wanted to know. "I feel like I'm missing something huge here."

"You are, Benny."

That wasn't Coach, it was Eliza. Her voice had rung out from behind me, so I spun around.

What's she doing here?

I had no idea, but even more confusing was why she was standing there with a baby in her arms.

21

BENNY, MEET AVA

ELIZA

With his mouth agape, Benny couldn't tear his gaze from me. Or rather, he couldn't tear his gaze from the baby in my arms.

When he recovered from his initial shock, he said, "Eliza, what's this all about? Whose baby is that?"

I took a step toward him. I was glad Ava was sleeping. She had woken up when I first roused her but had fallen back asleep during the car ride to the arena.

"This is Ava," I said softly, so as not to wake her. "I thought it was about time you met her."

He eyed my daughter warily, and then, in a near-whisper, he asked, "Ava is who to you, exactly?"

His eyes told me he already knew, but I answered him anyway.

Thinking *to hell with Drew*, I stated clearly, "She's my daughter, Benny."

My dad, who'd been quiet and content to let this play out, barked out a loud cough. He obviously had already figured out Benny had no idea I had a child.

Ignoring Dad, I smiled at Benny. "Would you like to hold her?"

Still looking rather stunned, he murmured an uneasy, "Okay."

I walked over to him and gently transferred Ava from my arms to his.

"I'm so sorry," I whispered to him. "It was wrong of me not to tell you about her."

"Why didn't you?" he murmured.

"I was afraid, at first. I just didn't want to scare you away. But then, there were...other reasons."

He raised a brow, but I shook my head. We could discuss things in more detail later.

But I had one thing to say that couldn't wait. "I hope you can forgive me, Benny."

He didn't reply one way or the other. He was too busy staring down at the baby in his arms. I stepped back to give him some space, and I could've melted right there. Big Benny was cradling my daughter like she was a fragile carton of eggs. She hadn't woken up. In fact, she seemed more content than ever. She was moving her legs a little and leaning her head against Benny's chest.

God, I hoped and prayed he would forgive me. I wanted him in my life, especially now witnessing him with Ava. I could see a real future with him. A future that became even clearer when Ava woke up and, instead of crying, peered up at Benny. She seemed fascinated by the gentle giant holding her.

Benny began rocking and cooing to Ava, melting me further into a puddle of goo. Images of a possible life with him flashed through my mind. I imagined Benny standing with me as we watched Ava take her first steps. And then I saw us waving, seeing Ava off on her first day of school.

I thought about what life would be like if this all worked out, and I saw happiness and…love.

Oh my God, I loved Benny.

I choked back a sob, and Benny's head jerked up.

"Am I doing it wrong?" He carefully adjusted Ava in his arms. "She looks okay, but am I hurting her?"

"God, no, Benny," I replied. "You're doing everything perfectly."

My dad, whom I'd almost forgotten was in the room, cleared his throat. Rising from behind his desk, he walked over to where Benny was holding Ava.

With a loving grandfatherly caress to Ava's cheek, he said to me softly, "I'm going to step into the office next door to give you guys some space. If Ava gets fussy just bring her to me."

"Thanks, Dad," I replied.

I was genuinely happy my plan had worked. My dad had forgotten—at least, for now—about chastising Benny.

"Yeah, thanks, Coach," Benny added.

He patted Benny on the shoulder, and then left.

The fact that he was leaving us alone spoke volumes. I knew then that if Benny chose to stick around—which I prayed he would—my dad would not de-ball him.

He'd be watching, though, of that I had no doubt.

Once we were alone, Benny asked, "Why were you so afraid to tell me about Ava?"

I took a deep breath. "Like I said before, I was scared you'd see me differently."

"What does that even mean? This is the twenty-first century, Eliza. There are no scarlet letters being passed out."

"Maybe not," I replied. "But that doesn't mean there aren't men out there who won't date a woman with a child."

"That's stupid," he said. "And besides, *I* don't think like that."

"No, you don't, and thank God for that."

He ran a hand over his head, still cradling Ava carefully. "I would never have viewed you any differently," he reiterated. "I've always liked you for you, Eliza. Knowing you had a baby wouldn't have changed my feelings, even from the start."

I loved hearing that, but I couldn't help but ask, "Are you absolutely sure?"

"Yes, I'm certain beyond a doubt."

I believed him, but I suspected he'd feel differently if he knew *who* Ava's father was. I couldn't tell him that part. Not only did Benny hate the guy, but I feared what Drew would do if I revealed his secret.

Other worries began to creep in, too. Just because Benny was standing there now, claiming he would've accepted Ava, it didn't mean he'd forgiven me for keeping her a secret for so long.

I was about to ask him where we stood on that issue when suddenly, like it had just dawned on him, he said, "Hey, wait a minute. That was Ava's pacifier that was stuck in the sofa cushions that day, wasn't it?"

"Um…"

He eyed me suspiciously. "It was, eh?"

"Yes," I admitted, "it was hers."

"Eliza," he sighed. "Is that baby food diet you told me about even real? Or have I been running around sucking on a pacifier and looking like a tool for nothing?"

"Maybe not," I hedged. "You said yourself that it helped with your donut cravings."

"Eliza..." It was a warning—no more lies.

So I fessed up. "Okay. There is no baby food diet. I made it up when you saw all that baby food in my cart. And there's no behavior modification supplemental program, either. It was the only thing I could think of to explain the pacifier."

I expected him to be angry, but he just started laughing.

"I suspected as much when Dylan had never heard of it. Nor could he find it on-line. I figured you'd just made it up...for whatever reason...and I kind of forgot about it. But you know what?"

"Uh-oh," I said quietly, "what?"

"Maybe the pacifier part *should* be in a plan. That damn thing's really helped me stay away from donuts."

"Maybe we're onto something," I said, smiling.

I was shocked he was taking it so well. Thrilled, but shocked.

"You're not mad at me, then?" I questioned.

"Shit, no."

He suddenly looked aghast. Peering down at Ava, he murmured in a hushed tone, "I'm sorry. I didn't mean to swear just now."

Laughing, and feeling so much relief I was giddy, I replied, "Benny, Ava's far too young to pick up on curse words. You're fine."

He nodded. "That's good, but I still think I should work on curbing my cursing. I'd hate to be a bad influence on her down the road."

Down the road? That boded well.

Still, I held my breath when I meekly asked, "Does that mean you still want me?"

"Of course I want you, Eliza. None of this stuff could lessen my feelings for you. I understand why you were afraid to tell me about

Ava. But the fact you didn't doesn't make me love you any less."

We both froze.

"What did you just say?" I whispered.

He squared up his shoulders and adjusted Ava in his arms. He was getting more comfortable with holding her. What was even cuter was I swear Ava, who was still awake and alert, was peering up at him like she was also waiting for him to repeat what he'd said.

And then he did. "I love you, Eliza. And I'm sure I'll love Ava soon enough, as well."

My heart soared. I wanted to jump into his arms, but Ava was already there.

"I love you, too, Benny," I replied.

He laughed. "Guess we're in for it now, eh?"

"Looks like we are," I concurred.

He leaned down and kissed me, and that was all I needed to know that it would all turn out okay.

I just hoped Drew didn't interfere.

A WARNING

BENNY

I meant what I'd said to Eliza—I loved her. And I planned to stick around. I wouldn't have felt any differently had I known about Ava from the start. But it didn't matter now. I knew, and I still wanted to be with Eliza for the long haul.

We were still hanging out in Coach's office when Ava got a little fussy. I guess she'd had enough of me. Eliza took her back, and we readied to leave.

But then, as we were stepping out into the hallway, Coach T yelled out from the office next door, "Come in here, Perry. I'd like to speak with you alone for a minute."

I side-eyed Eliza. "Uh-oh, that can't be good."

She begged to differ. "I think you're okay in my dad's book. He left us alone in his office, right?"

"He did."

"Then he can't be *that* against the idea of us."

"Ha, if that's true, it's only because Ava softened him up."

Laughing and peering down at the little girl in her arms, she said, "That was the plan, Benny. That's why I brought her along with me. Plus"—she gave me a sweet smile—"I wanted you to finally meet her."

"I'm glad you did, Eliza."

Coach yelled for me again, and I said, "I better get in there."

"Yeah, go." She laughed. "Take your lumps like a man."

I assumed she was teasing and there'd be no lumps doled out. Just in case, I covered my nuts as I opened the door.

"Why are you just standing there, Perry?" Coach T grumbled when I lingered. "Are you coming in or not?"

"I am, I am."

Uncovering my junk, I made my way to a chair opposite him.

"I'm assuming you're sticking around?" he began, getting right to the point as he steepled his hands on the desktop.

"Yes, I plan to stay with Eliza."

He released a long breath. "That's good to hear. Since, for whatever reason, my daughter seems to like you quite a bit."

"Thank you, sir. I think I've made it clear that I like her quite a bit, too."

"Hmm..." He gave me an assessing once-over. "You've changed a lot this past year."

"I have, sir."

"Nevertheless, I'm not completely sure you're the right guy for my girl."

"Hey!"

He held up a hand. "Give me a minute, I'm not done."

Contrite, I replied, "Sorry, sir."

"What I'm trying to say is that I'm willing to give you a chance, for Eliza's sake."

"Thank you," I replied, feeling pretty darn good.

"Don't look so smug, Benny. If I ever hear you're back to your old ways—"

"Whoa, wait." I had to cut him off and set him straight. "Let me assure you that will *never* happen. I'd never hurt Eliza, I promise you that."

He warned, "You better not."

23

NOT YOU, UGH!

ELIZA

It hadn't been an act in my dad's office. Nor was it a one-time fluke. Benny really was all right with Ava. And amazing with her, too.

I was thrilled to find that Ava *adored* him. It was just as heartening to discover Benny was a fast learner. He caught on right away when I taught him how to hold Ava properly.

"Was I doing it wrong in your dad's office?" he inquired as he shifted her to a more suitable position. "My sister has a baby, but I don't get to see her much."

"No, no, you're doing really well," I assured him. "Always be sure to support her head, though."

"Ah, got it."

He did, in fact, get it, and I laughed. "See, you're a natural."

"You bet I am, babe."

I showed him how to burp Ava next. He got that one down, but she spit up on him in the process.

"Ugh, disgusting." He held her away from him while orange-y brown goo dripped down the front of his shirt.

Ava had just eaten the infamous sweet potatoes she loved so much, and Benny was now wearing them. Gross as it was, I couldn't help but snicker.

"Better get used to it," I said. "Babies do that all the time."

Passing Ava back to me and grabbing a bunch of wipes to clean up, he remarked, "This just made it official."

"What's that?"

"I will never, *ever* touch anything labeled 'sweet potato' again in my life."

I made a sad face. "Aw, not even our favorite tart?"

"Not even, Eliza. I will never again look at any tart without remembering this day, the day I wore regurgitated slop."

Next lesson up was teaching Benny how to discern if Ava had had enough food or formula. He learned that one the fastest.

"Less chance of getting puked on again," he gave as his reason.

And then came the final task, the coup de grâce—showing him how to change a diaper. That one was the funniest, especially the first time he tried.

"Holy shit, Eliza! What the fuck happened in here?" Benny was horrified and holding his nose upon encountering his first poopy diaper.

"She took a crap, Benny." I rolled my eyes. "What did you expect, a bouquet of roses?"

"Well, no, not roses, but...daaamn."

He backed away, and I had to take over from there.

"I'm just wondering how someone so small can make so much," he marveled.

Laughing, I informed him, "This one isn't even that bad. You should see it after she eats too much of that banana baby food she likes."

"Ugh, I can imagine. And I don't even want to think about the sweet potato ones. They were bad enough coming out the other way."

I assured him, "Yep, you don't want to know how bad those can be, Benny."

I counted him out for diaper duty. But I was wrong. The next time Ava needed a diaper changed, he dove right in.

Still intent on holding his nose and maintaining the whole time that baby poop was "frighteningly god-awful," he got the hang of it in no time and was soon changing diapers like an old pro.

"You're no longer a rookie," I informed him.

"Good to hear," he deadpanned. "I've officially moved from a confirmed playboy to a seasoned veteran diaper changer."

"You have indeed, Mr. Perry," I replied. "You've come a long way."

"I have."

Later that same day we had to head over to the arena to drop off paperwork for my dad. He'd accidentally left a sealed folder of documents at the house and he needed them right away.

I had a feeling the paperwork had to do with a secret trade coming up.

With Nolan out of the line-up, the team had fallen into a bit of a slump. Ownership wanted to shake things up. There'd been talk of a lateral trade, maybe a right winger for another right winger.

That'd work out perfectly since Nolan Solvenson's wrist injury had turned out to be much worse than originally thought. Although

Nolan was out for the time being, he'd be back and there was no chance of him being traded. He was just too valuable to the team. Plus, the Wolves had a decent third-line right winger they could deal. That guy was playing far below his level and hadn't been happy for a while. My dad had moved him up to the first line following Nolan's injury, but he, Brent, and Benny just weren't working out.

It was time for a change. Too bad the big folder we were taking to my father was sealed.

"Damn," Benny said as we walked into the sports complex. "I bet we could find out who the team is looking at if we break that seal."

"Benny," I warned, "that is *not* a good idea. My dad will see the packet's been tampered with."

Since I had Ava, he was in possession of the papers. With a devious grin, he held up the folder and said, "We could always reseal it."

I had Ava in one of those baby pouches, so my hands were free. Good thing for that, as I was able to snatch the folder from a far-too-curious Benny.

"Hey," he protested. "I wasn't *really* going to open it."

"Better safe than sorry," I replied.

We were at the end of the hall and making the turn to where the elevators were located.

That's when I almost ran smack-dab into a guy as big as Benny. Strong hands landed on my shoulder, keeping me from stumbling with Ava.

"Oh, I'm sorry," I stammered, stepping way the hell back.

There was something oddly familiar about the guy, even before I looked up at his face.

When I did raise my head, I muttered, "Shit."

Benny didn't hear me. He was too busy shooting daggers at the man. No surprise there, seeing as it was none other than his nemesis—Drew Chidders.

Kill me now.

Fuck, I have Ava with me.

Good thing Drew was fully engaged in a testosterone-laden standoff with Benny. Their gazes were locked, meaning he hadn't noticed I was the girl who'd almost walked into him.

It gave me a minute to think, plus put on my best game face.

"Perry," he snapped.

Benny nodded curtly, growling a none-too-friendly, "Chidders."

All I could think was, *why in the hell is Drew Chidders in Las Vegas?* God, I prayed it had nothing to do with the impending trade.

The guys gave up on their dick-measuring contest and Drew finally took a good look at me. But shockingly, I received little more than a flickering glance. It was Ava who garnered his full attention.

It was the first time he'd ever laid eyes on her, and even Iceman was affected. I wasn't fooled, however. I knew this fascination with her would only be temporary. Drew was just too into himself.

Ava was already pressed close to my breast, where she was still sleeping. I now brought my arms up to hold on to her more securely. I didn't know why Drew was at the home of the Wolves, and really, I didn't care. If he became a part of the team, so be it. I just didn't want him anywhere near Ava. He hadn't earned that right. He hadn't even earned the right to lay his slimy eyes on her—though that's what he was doing—not after the way he'd behaved on our last phone call.

The things he'd said—calling his daughter a *distraction*, threatening to take her away. An especially heinous act since he hadn't ever publicly acknowledged she was his.

I fumed just thinking about it, but I needed to stay cool.

Despite the well-known rivalry between the two men, it was Benny who proved to be the better man. He stepped back and introduced us.

Talk about awkward. Benny didn't know my history with Drew, or that *he* was Ava's freaking father.

I prayed it wouldn't blow up in my face when I said to Drew, "Uh, it's nice to meet you."

Dickhead stuck out his hand, smug grin firmly in place. "Likewise, *Eliza*."

My hand shook like a leaf when I reluctantly took his. Drew loved every second of it. He was smirking when, instead of shaking and letting go, he raised my hand to his mouth and kissed the back.

I jerked away like I'd been burned. "Uh, so, yeah, no."

Benny peered over at me, no doubt confused by my gibberish.

I just shrugged.

For the first time ever, I was actually glad when jackass Drew opened his mouth, even if it was to mockingly state, "What a cute baby you have there, Eliza."

His prick comment gave me a reprieve on having to explain to Benny why I was behaving so strangely.

In a tight voice, I ground out a curt, "Thank you, Drew."

He wasn't done with his twisted fun.

Even though Benny was staring at him, Drew ignored him, and went on to ask me, "May I hold her?"

What? He's kidding, right?

"Huh?" I was caught way the hell off guard. "You want to hold Ava?"

"Yes, I'd like to hold her. Ava is such a pretty name, by the way."

"Dude." Benny shook his head, more perplexed than ever.

Drew again ignored Benny and asked me, this time with his arms outstretched, "So may I hold her?"

He was such an assuming asshole. But truthfully I was torn. He was her father, after all.

But when he smirked, like this was all a game to him, and not a nice one at that, I made up my mind.

Not here, not now, my eyes conveyed when he looked at me again.

Then, in a very clear voice, I said, "As you can see, Ava's sleeping. She should really just rest. She was fussy earlier, so I think it's for the best that she stays with me."

That last line meant so much more, and Drew knew it.

Glaring at me, he snapped, "Funny, I don't see a father around." He glanced dismissively at Benny, knowing full well he had no children. "Maybe not having a dad in her life is why your baby gets fussy to begin with."

That no-good, absentee-father prick! Is he really going to play it this way?

Apparently he was, and I knew then that he'd do whatever it took to hurt me, all because he didn't like—and was clearly jealous of—Benny. Drew didn't want me, but he sure as hell didn't want his biggest adversary to have me either.

Too bad for him, Benny was in my life for good.

"Dude, what the fuck is your problem?" Benny chimed in.

"You want to know what my problem is?" Drew snickered.

"Yes," Benny replied, "I do."

I couldn't imagine Drew disclosing that he was Ava's dad, not after all the carrying on about keeping his identity a secret. But one could never be sure with him. Seeing Ava in person had affected him, even if he was being a dickhead about it. The fact that he couldn't keep his eyes off her for more than a minute told me all I needed to know. And

I didn't like the implications.

Terrified of what it all might mean—like, would Drew fight me for Ava?—I grabbed Benny's hand.

"Sorry," I said, urging Benny to play along by squeezing firmly. "We really need to get going."

"Yeah, we do," Benny confirmed.

Thank you, thank you.

Drew stood there, a scowl on his face, as Benny let me lead him to an elevator that was thankfully open.

As he pressed the button so the doors would close, he murmured, "Wow, that guy is even weirder than I thought."

"Yeah." I pretended to laugh. "He sure is."

"I wonder what he's doing here," Benny mused.

"You don't think he's part of this"—I waved the folder in my hand—"proposed trade package, do you?"

Benny looked at the folder and frowned. "Crap, he could be, Eliza. Are you sure you still don't want to take a peek?"

I shook my head. "No, we'd better not."

Truth was I'd had enough of Drew Chidders. I didn't need to open the file. I suspected he was indeed part of the trade, a trade that would bring him to Las Vegas. That certainly explained his cocky behavior minutes before.

What was I going to do?

With the way Drew had acted, I wondered how much longer he'd keep it a secret that he was Ava's father, especially living in the same town.

There was good and bad to that possibility. And it raised a lot of questions.

Should I tell Benny now?

Or should I ease him into it by first divulging that I slept with Drew?

That probably won't go over well, especially after today. Maybe I should hold off and see how things play out.

Crap, I wasn't sure what to do.

So I did the worst thing possible—absolutely nothing.

PRICK MEET FIST

BENNY

I discovered soon enough why Drew Chidders was at the Desert Sports Complex. And it was what I had suspected—the prick had been traded to our team in return for that third-line right winger that hadn't been working out. In other words, it was my worst nightmare, come true.

But things were worse than I ever could have imagined.

"Until Nolan returns, he's on *our* line," Brent informed me in the locker room before the start of practice the morning after the news of the trade had broken.

"Fuck," I muttered. "This is going to be absolute misery. I hate that motherfucker."

"Get over it, Benny. I'm no fan of his either, but he's our teammate now and we have to make it work."

Brent was right, so I said, "I know. We need to find some kind of chemistry with that tool."

It was the truth. Without Nolan the Wolves's slump had continued straight through the holidays. Not only were we sliding in the standings, but it was January, the time of year when teams really buckled down.

"We're halfway through the season," Brent said. "We have no choice but to find a way to turn things around."

I didn't know if Drew would be the answer, but I was willing to make peace with him for the sake of our team.

Too bad he didn't feel the same way.

Within the first five minutes of that initial practice, he was checking me into the boards, and saying weird-ass shit like, "You think you're better than me, Perry? Just remember, I was there first."

"Huh?"

I finally had enough and skated to a stop, spraying his ass with snow. "What the fuck, Chidders? You got something to say, just spit it out."

He slipped his helmet off and ran his hand through his mop of dark brown hair, wet from sweat.

I could see he was dying to tell me something, so I pressed, "What's your deal, man?"

Leaning on his stick, he spat, "You want to know my deal, *man*?"

"I sure as shit do."

"That girl you're with—"

"Wait, who? Eliza?"

He nodded. "Yeah, her."

I bristled, not liking his all-too-knowing smirk. "What about her?" I snapped.

He started skating backward.

And then he began to laugh. Grabbing his junk, he said, "I bet she hasn't told you that *I* was with her before you knew her. Hey, I can't blame you for wanting to hit that shit. That sexy bitch is one hell of a lay."

That was it. "You motherfucker!"

I threw off my helmet and went for him, fists flying. I didn't care that he was my new teammate. I didn't care about working together. What he had spewed was over the line.

Was it true, though?

Could that be why Eliza had acted so strangely when we'd run into him?

My focus on Drew sputtered.

He saw an opening and went for it, clipping me on the jaw.

"Fucking prick," I bit out.

I was about to throw a blow of my own, but I never had the chance. Our teammates had noticed we were fighting and were now rushing over to pull us apart.

It was actually good they'd gotten to us before the coaching staff had. Coach Townsend and his assistants were still in the back having a meeting.

After Drew and I were separated, I was seething, seeing red and nothing else.

"What the hell was that all about?" I heard Dylan say.

As I calmed down, I realized he was the guy leading me off the ice.

I angled to turn around and go at Chidders again. "I got one more thing to say to him," I said to Dylan as I tried to skate away.

He was having none of it.

"Enough, Benny," he warned, grabbing a fistful of my practice jersey and corralling me back.

Brent was leading Drew to the locker room, up ahead of us. So, not surprisingly, Dylan steered me to a nearby lounge.

Once he shut the door behind us, I sat down on a chair and put my head in my hands. "This is so fucked-up," I grumbled.

"Want to tell me what the hell just happened out there?" Dylan asked.

I was still processing what Chidders had said, and I didn't like the implications I was coming up with.

"Why wouldn't she tell me?" I muttered, confused six ways to Sunday about Eliza.

"Tell you what?" Dylan pulled up a chair and sat across from me. "Are we talking about Eliza? Is that what that fight was about? What did that asshole say to you out there?"

"Fuck, man. It's so bad I don't even want to repeat it."

"How bad could it be?" Dylan shrugged. "Does he know someone who slept with her or something?"

I leveled him a look, and he got it. "Shit. *He* slept with her?"

Sighing, I filled him in.

"Yeah, apparently he did sleep with her. I just don't know why she wouldn't tell me herself. She knows that prick's on our team now. And she's more than aware he and I can't stand each other."

"Maybe that's why she didn't say anything." Dylan raised a brow.

"Yeah," I sighed. "I guess that would make sense."

I didn't hold it against Eliza that she'd had the bad judgment to sleep with, of all the men in the world, Drew fucking Chidders. But I couldn't help but wonder why she hadn't trusted me enough to share.

"What'd she think?" I muttered. "Was she worried I'd fly into a jealous rage?"

Nodding to my bruised and bloodied fists, Dylan said, "Yeah, 'cause that would never happen, huh?"

That made me laugh. "Dude, you are such a dick."

Standing and clapping me on the back, he reminded me, "Just remember that I'm the dick who got you off the ice before Coach T came out."

He had a point. "True."

I acted like everything was fine, but things were far from good. I was burned that Eliza hadn't told me about Drew. Her keeping it a secret made me feel like a fool. She had to know Drew would eventually use it to bait me. It sure hadn't taken long.

But there was more.

I didn't like that this was the *third* time she'd kept something from me. I wasn't much concerned about the diet and pacifier silliness, but not telling me about Ava bothered me now. I'd forgiven her so easily for her transgressions, yet now there was this.

Sleeping with goddamn Drew Chidders?

It made me wonder how many more secrets Eliza was keeping.

That was it—I needed to talk to her. I was starting to feel like I could use a little space. Had we moved too quickly? Graham thought we had, though he'd never outright say it to me. I knew it weighed on him, though. He wanted me with someone who was good for me.

Was Eliza good for me?

I thought so, but maybe I was wrong. I was getting into fights with freaking teammates, for fuck's sake. Maybe I'd gotten it all wrong about her.

I felt like I'd come so far in so many ways, battling old demons and all that. I didn't want to get caught up in a toxic relationship, especially not one built on distrust.

And that begged the question—could I really *trust* Eliza?

25

SECRETS BITE ME IN THE ASS

ELIZA

Benny called me on his way home from practice and asked me I could meet him at his house.

"As soon as possible, Eliza," he said, sounding uncharacteristically cool and aloof. "It's important."

I knew then that something was up. I also had a feeling I knew what had caused Benny's distress—Drew Chidders.

That morning had been their first practice together. And from the way Drew had behaved when he ran into me and Benny at the Desert Sports Complex, I didn't put anything past him.

Cursing him out all the way to Benny's house, I prepared for the worst. I suspected it would be bad. And then I knew it for sure when I pulled into Benny's driveway and found him waiting for me, arms crossed and looking none too happy.

I tried to throw him off, ease him up a little, when I hopped out of my car and flashed him my best smile. "Hey, Benny. How's it going?"

He nodded curtly. "Hello, Eliza."

Damn, even the cute sundress I'd purposely worn wasn't working. The scowl on his face didn't wane in the slightest.

I decided to drop the cutesy act and cut to the chase.

"What's up?" I asked in a somber tone. "Why did you want me to come over?"

"To talk," he stated flatly.

"Okay."

He motioned to the house. "I think we should go inside."

"Sure, all right."

Once we were in the foyer, it took only thirty seconds for my world to fall apart.

"Did you sleep with Drew Chidders?" Benny asked, turning to me, brow raised.

Crap, we hadn't even made it to the living room.

"Uh," I so eloquently murmured.

Thankfully, there was a chair handy. I sat down—or more sort of crumpled—onto it.

After hearing Benny's to-the-point question, my legs were shaky, leaving me with the option of either sitting…or crumpling to the floor in shame.

I'd chosen sitting. And though my body grew numb, my mind started racing.

Benny knows about me and Drew.

He knows we had sex.

Drew freaking told him.

Crap, how much more did that jerk say?

Does Benny know Ava is Drew's daughter?

It seemed not, or he would've led with that.

"Eliza, are you going to answer my question?" Benny asked exasperatedly. "Or do you plan on sitting there all day in a daze."

"Um, I, uh…" I put my head in my hands. "I just don't know what to say," I whispered.

"How about the fucking truth," Benny yelled, making my head shoot up. "For once, don't feed me a line of bullshit."

I'd never seen him this upset off the ice.

"I'm sorry, Benny. I'm so sorry," I kept repeating.

"It's true, isn't it?" he said, at last. "Drew wasn't fucking lying." He swiped his hand down his face. "Fuck! I am such a fool. And there I was, hoping the whole way here that that fucker was just being his usual prick self."

"I slept with him," I admitted, "it's true. I wish it had never happened, but it did. I can't change the past, Benny, but I *can* say I'm sorry."

I hung my head in shame. Not for having slept with Drew, as it happened long before I'd ever known Benny. I was simply ashamed that I'd not told him myself. I'd been so worried that telling him would lead to sharing that I got pregnant with Ava.

Yet here we were.

Oh, hell, I'd just tell him everything now, the whole story.

But it seemed Benny had questions first. Ones like, "How many times did it happen?"

"I don't know exactly. It was more than once, I can tell you that."

He groaned, like that was the last thing he'd wanted to hear.

"I just don't understand why you would sleep with *him*, especially more than once. He's such an asshole."

"I couldn't agree more."

He threw his hands up. "So why'd you do it?"

"I wasn't thinking at the time," I exclaimed, exasperated.

He snorted, but I went on. "I saw only what I wanted to see, Benny. Stuff I hoped was true. I liked Drew, and I convinced myself he was someone he wasn't. It wasn't until much later that I saw the real him and realized he's a complete tool."

"That's an understatement," he scoffed.

"Benny."

I blew out a breath, and he reiterated, "You should've told me. Especially after you knew he'd been traded to our team."

"I know. You're absolutely right."

He was, too. But I could fix it all now. I'd share every sordid detail, including that Ava was Drew's daughter.

This was it, the moment had arrived. I stood and went to Benny, ready to tell him *everything*. Damn the consequences.

Benny, with no idea of my intentions, held out his hand, thus stopping me in my tracks.

"No, Eliza." He shook his head. I'd never seen him more resigned. "I know what you're doing."

"You do?"

"Yes. You think we can just kiss and make up. But not everything can be solved with sex." He scrubbed his hand down his face. "Shit, I can't believe I'm saying that."

"Wait." I wrung my hands. "I'm not trying to solve anything with sex. I just want to talk. There's more I need to tell you. It's important."

He shook his head. "I really don't care. Not anymore."

Ouch. "I don't believe that," I murmured, stunned.

"Believe or not, I just can't hear anything more you have to say right now."

"Okay. But I need to tell you at least one th—"

"No, Eliza. I'm serious." His eyes met mine, and I could tell he wasn't kidding around. "I'm done talking about this. In fact, I'm just plain fucking done."

I was floored. "Wait? What do you mean you're done?"

"It means I can't be in this relationship with you. We're over. I need openness and honesty, and I'm not getting that from you. I haven't for a while."

Frustrated, I threw up my hands. "I'm *trying* to be open and honest now. You just won't let me. You don't want to hear anything more I have to say."

"That's right, I don't. It's too late, babe."

I tried again to confess that Ava was Drew's child. But I got no further than, "Benny, just let me come clean about one thing—"

"No, stop. You should just leave, Eliza." He opened the door, motioning for me to be on my way.

There was no point in saying another word, so I did what he wanted me to do—I left.

26

SO EFFING DONE... MAYBE

BENNY

Ah, Eliza. She kept insisting she had more to tell me, but I was just so fucking done. Just the image of her and Drew... Fuck. I couldn't even think about it.

It sucked that Drew was on our top line. But what could I do? I couldn't kick him off the team, or off our line, so I dug deep. I had to get along with him, at least on the ice.

And somehow, despite all the odds, over time it worked. Drew, Brent, and I actually gelled as a unit.

We started playing well together, and the team was soon back on track.

Though our communication was there on the ice, I barely spoke to Drew off of it. There were no more barbs from either of us, no more cheap verbal shots. We simply had nothing to say to one another.

I guessed he must've heard through the grapevine that whatever I'd had with Eliza was over and done.

But was it really, though?

It sure didn't feel like it. At least, it didn't when I peered into my heart and asked myself how I really felt about her.

I missed her, I couldn't lie.

I was sick of her lies, sure, but I kind of wanted her back. I felt like we could work on things. What could I say? The heart wants what the heart wants. Who ever said love was rational?

Unlike before, I didn't confide in anyone about anything. I just went about my business and played good hockey. I found that focusing on each game individually kept my mind occupied. It also kept me out of trouble.

I was determined not to let my failed relationship send me spiraling. I went to fuckloads of meetings as a precaution. That meant I saw Graham a lot. But I made sure I talked only about things other than my love life.

Graham must've assumed Eliza and I were still together, probably thought I was too busy with hockey to bring her up in a conversation. Hockey was pretty much all I ever talked about, so him thinking that made sense.

I gushed in copious detail about how it was great that the team was back in first place in the standings. And I rambled on and on about how we might really make another run for the Cup.

I wasn't the only one saying shit like that. There was a ton of scuttlebutt about the subject, people saying the Wolves could win back-to-back Stanley Cups.

Not wanting us distracted by what-ifs and maybes, Coach Townsend began limiting our press time.

"We need to stay focused, boys," he said to the team one morning after he'd put us through a particularly grueling practice. "We can't get sucked in by all this hype. It'll just be a distraction."

"He's right," Brent chimed in. "Let's take the next couple of months of regular-season hockey one game at a time."

"Here, here." I tapped my stick on the ice in solidarity, and the rest of the team joined in.

As we were heading to the locker room a few minutes later, Coach pulled me aside. "After you're cleaned up, come see me in my office," he said.

Fuck.

Had he discovered Eliza and I had gone our separate ways? He had to know. She lived at his house, for fuck's sake.

Worried I was in for a world of hurt from Coach—for breaking his little girl's heart or whatever—I showered in a daze. I threw on a dress shirt and some nice pants, and set off to take it like a man.

Rapping twice on Coach T's office door, I nervously announced, "Hey, it's me. Perry."

"Come on in," he called out from behind the closed door.

He sounded kind of cheery, which filled me with hope that whatever it was he wanted to talk about, maybe it wasn't too bad.

"Take a seat, Benjamin," he said when I ventured in.

He was being so formal. But based on the past, I wasn't sure if that was a good or bad sign.

Then I was thrown for a loop.

Just as I was sitting down, something caught my eye, something that made me not give a shit about Coach and his feelings towards me.

See, there was this framed picture on his desk, a photo of Eliza and Ava. Fuck, it truly felt like a stake had been driven through my heart. It hurt so much that I had to hold my chest.

I missed Eliza so damn much, but I hadn't realized that I'd missed Ava, as well. That little girl had stolen my heart.

And now I'd never see her again, except in photographs like the one on Coach's desk.

I should look away to pull myself together.

But I couldn't.

I'd been set to play it cool, but all I could do was shakily ask, "How are they doing, Coach T?"

He followed my gaze to the photo, and, sighing, said, "My granddaughter is doing great. And my daughter... Well, she's fine, considering."

Our eyes met, and I knew then that he knew.

Shit, I felt compelled to explain.

"Look, Coach, I have to tell you something. Obviously, you're aware that Eliza and I are no longer together. But that doesn't mean I don't care about her...and Ava." My voice cracked. "I hope you can find it in your heart to believe me when I say I never intended to hurt Eliza."

"That's enough." He waved his hand around. "I don't need to hear this. A part of me would like to ream you out. But I made a promise to my wife that I'd stay out of it...and I'm going to. Whatever happened between you and Eliza, it's none of my business. And it's definitely not why I called you up to my office today."

Huh? "That's not the reason?"

"No, it's not."

"Okay."

He cleared his throat. "As you know, Nolan Solvenson is out. What you may not have heard yet is that he needs surgery on his injured wrist."

"What?" Coach was right, I hadn't heard. Shit, this was bad.

"That means he'll be out for at least two more months," Coach said.

"No way..." I was aghast. "That means he won't be back till the playoffs start."

"Assuming we make it that far," Coach stated grimly.

I felt strongly that no matter what we would make it, leading me to say, "Oh, we will."

Playing great hockey on an amazingly talented team was the one sure thing I had in my life. So I *had* to be right, damn it.

"We're going to make it," I repeated, more adamantly. "If for nothing else, so that Nolan gets a chance to play once more this season."

Coach smiled. "I like your attitude, Perry. And I have to say, you've really grown into the player and leader I always knew you could be."

"Wow." I was speechless.

"In fact, it's your leadership as of late, especially with Nolan being out, that has you in my office today."

"It is?"

I was oblivious to where this was going. Or rather, I was until Coach opened a drawer in his desk and pulled out a black and red Wolves jersey with *my* name and number on it.

When he passed it over to me and I saw the letter "A" sewn on the front, I knew then exactly why I was there.

"You want *me* to be an assistant captain?"

Coach laughed. "Bet you never saw that one coming. And, yes, I do."

"Can't say that I did," I admitted, still stunned.

"Don't look so surprised. Like I said before, you've become a real team leader."

All I could do was stare and stare at that jersey. I even fucking started tearing up.

"This is a real honor, Coach," I choked out. "Thank you."

"You've earned it," he said. "You should also know you've finally earned my respect."

"Thank you, sir. That means a lot."

I couldn't believe *those* words had come out of Coach's mouth. And it did mean a lot, like I'd told him, but it would've meant more had I still been with Eliza.

I'd wanted Coach's blessing so badly, and now I had it.

Too bad it was too late.

27

LIFE WITHOUT BENNY

ELIZA

Benny didn't want to hear the truth. I knew I'd waited too long to offer it up to him. I didn't want the same thing to happen with Lainey, so I decided to tell her everything as soon as possible.

We met for margaritas at a cute little Mexican bistro that was near my house. I obviously didn't take Ava, but I sure brought lots of pictures of her, photos I'd printed and planned to show Lainey. I intended to tell her what happened with Benny, as well. And of course, how *I'd* fucked things up.

I didn't care what Drew would do, not anymore. My accountability for my own actions had become more important. Keeping secrets—for myself and for him—had left me stranded on an island.

But I was ready to paddle back to shore.

I arrived at the bistro before Lainey and secured us a spot far away from everyone. Once I was seated at a corner booth, I ordered a margarita, knowing I'd need alcohol to kick off the conversation we were about to have.

Still, I felt like I needed more than that. So, before the waiter left, I said, "May I have an extra shot of tequila in my margarita?"

"Certainly, miss," he replied.

And then he was gone.

Lainey arrived a few minutes later. When I saw how beautiful she looked I teasingly whistled at her. She was wearing a cute purple dress and her beautiful raven hair was pinned up.

"Look at you, sexy mama," I said when she sat down across from me. "No one will ever accuse married life of not agreeing with you."

She laughed, and replied, "I do have to say, I love being Mrs. Nolan Solvenson."

"Ah, love…" I sighed.

I'd been so close to having that and more with Benny, till I screwed it up by hiding too many truths.

Well, no more.

I was about to bust out the pictures of Ava right there, but the waiter had returned with my margarita and a huge basket of warm chips and salsa.

Lainey dug in immediately, proclaiming, "I'm freaking starving."

"Hmm, let's see, radiant and starving… Holy crap, you're not pregnant, are you?"

Poor Lainey almost choked on a chip.

Once she recovered, she said, "God, no. And after that statement"—she beckoned the waiter over—"I think I need a drink."

Pointing to my margarita, she said to the waiter, "I'll have one of those."

"Certainly, miss," he replied. "Would you like extra tequila in yours, as well?"

She looked at me and raised a brow.

I shrugged, and she said, "Sure, why not."

After the waiter left, Lainey leaned back.

"This is nice, Eliza, a night out with no guys. We need to do this more often."

"Definitely," I agreed. "It's been way too long."

She nodded. "It has."

Her margarita arrived, and we spent the next half hour drinking and catching up on all the little things. I'd reveal my secret soon enough.

"How's school?" Lainey asked at one point.

"Really good," I replied. "I'm back on track to graduate on time, so this is definitely going to be my last semester."

"That's fantastic, Eliza." Lainey rubbed her hands together. "Enough about school, though. Let's get to the good stuff."

"Yeah, like what?"

"First off, how're things on the 'ole love life front?"

I coughed. "What love life front?"

"Wait." Lainey looked confused. "I thought after seeing that cute pic of you and Benny that something was going on with you two."

"There was something going on," I admitted. "But it's over now."

Her brows shot up. "Already?"

Here we go…

"Actually, that 'something going on' was going on for a while."

She narrowed her eyes, but not in any kind of angry way. She simply looked hurt. "Why didn't you tell me, Eliza?"

"Well, Benny and I, we, uh—"

"Hold up." Lainey raised her hand. "Before you say another word, tell me now, did that bastard cheat on you? Is that why you're no longer together?"

Before I could answer, she exclaimed, "Oh my God. He did, didn't he? Crap, Eliza, I told you he was a player. Damn him."

"Lainey, it's not like th—"

"Do you want me to kick him in the balls for you? I can make it lethal if need be. Just ask Nolan."

"Whoa," I blurted out, "poor Nolan."

She assured me she'd never hurt her man. "I love him too much," she said.

Worried for Benny's balls, though, I felt compelled to say, "Benny was actually really amazing. He didn't cheat on me. I was the one who fucked up."

Her big turquoise eyes widened. "*You* cheated on *him*?"

"No, it wasn't that. It was another kind of deception."

"Hmm, sounds like there's a story there. Shit, how have I missed all this? I feel like the world's suckiest friend right now."

"It's not you, Lainey. It's me." I sighed, took a sip of my drink. "There's so much you don't know, things you should. That's why I'm about to tell you *everything*."

I shared all my secrets then. I told Lainey how much I was into Benny from that very first hockey game, the one when she and I first met. I also explained how there'd been this crazy chemistry brewing from the start, one we couldn't—and didn't—ignore.

"I noticed that early on," she said. "I used to say to Nolan all the time that we should hook you two up. Hell, I told you as much, too."

"Yeah, you did. You were so rah-rah about us at first. What happened?"

She sighed. "Nolan filled me in on how Benny was a major player. He told me about the puck bunny directory, and, well, like I said on the phone that day, I just didn't want to see you get hurt."

"That was sweet of you, Lainey." My voice cracked. "But here I sit, heartbroken. Too bad it wasn't Benny who tore us apart."

Softly, she said, "Eliza, what the hell happened?"

Putting my head in my hands, I said, "I fucked up so badly, Lainey."

"I can't imagine how."

Looking up and meeting her gaze, I blurted out, "I slept with Drew Chidders. That's how."

Her face paled. "Wait, I thought you said you didn't cheat on Benny?"

"I didn't. It happened long before I ever met him."

She looked confused. "Why would he break up with you over that? I mean, I know he hates the guy, but with *his* past he has *no* room to judge."

I was tearing up, and I dabbed at my eyes with a cocktail napkin.

"He wasn't mad that it happened. Well, maybe a little," I clarified. "That wasn't what broke us up, though. What did it for him was that I kept it all a secret. He found out about it from Drew."

"That jerk!"

"Yeah, Drew Chidders can be really shitty sometimes. Still, I should've told Benny before it ever got to that point."

Lainey blew out a breath.

It was a lot to take in. And we'd just scratched the surface.

"I don't know, Eliza," she began. "It still doesn't seem like *that* awful of a thing."

Softly, I murmured, "That wasn't the first secret I'd kept from him."

"What else could there be?"

"Oh, just wait." I began to dig for the photos of Ava in my purse. When I had a heaping handful, I slid them across the table. "Here," I said. "I have a hundred more like these on my phone."

Lainey looked down at the photos and knew immediately there'd be only one reason why I'd have that many pictures of one particular child.

"Holy crap," she exclaimed, looking up. "This adorable baby is yours? Oh, Eliza, she's beautiful."

I couldn't help but smile. I felt like one proud mama.

"So what's her name?" Lainey asked.

"Ava."

"That's a pretty name," she murmured as she flipped through the many photos.

"Thank you. That little girl is just... She's my..." I searched for the right words, choking up when I finally found them. "Ava is everything to me."

Lainey smiled.

But then she began to frown.

"What's wrong?" I asked.

She ground out, "Don't even tell me Benny gave you a hard time about this beautiful child."

"No, no," I was quick to reply. "It was nothing like that. He actually took that news really well. He adores Ava. It was the Drew thing that put him over the top."

Lainey looked relieved. But then she peered over at me, like really intently.

"What now?" I asked.

Slowly, she shook her head. "I don't know, Eliza. The Drew-thing still isn't reason enough to end something good. And from all you've just told me, it sounds like what you and Benny had was the real deal."

I choked up. "It was."

"Then go get him, girl. Work this shit out."

"He doesn't want to talk to me."

"Oh, stop. Make him listen. I know you can."

"I would, but—"

"But nothing, Eliza. What's really holding you back?"

"There's one last secret," I confessed in a whisper. "And trust me, Lainey, this is something Benny will *never* forgive me for."

"I doubt that," she maintained. "Nothing could be that bad."

"It is. It's about Ava's father. The problem is *who* he is."

That slowed her go-get-Benny roll. "Um, who is he?"

This was hard. I was about to tell her something no one knew, not even my mom or dad. But I had to do it.

Voice cracking, I uttered for the first time ever out loud, "Drew Chidders is Ava's dad."

"Holy crap, Eliza! Fuck, shit, wow."

"Yeah, I pretty much feel the same way."

After she pulled herself together, she asked, "How'd you even meet him? He played in Dallas last year, right? And you were living in DC."

"I was, yeah. A friend of mine from Georgetown knew him from their hometown. Drew was up there visiting her that summer and she set us up. One thing led to another, and well, as they say, the rest is history."

"Ah, got it."

"It was really fun at first. He seemed so nice. He'd even fly back to see me after the season started. But then he suddenly ended things." I sighed. "I found out I was pregnant shortly thereafter. When I called and told him, he said he didn't care. He was done with me and stated that he wanted nothing more to do with me…or the baby."

"What about now?" she quietly inquired. "I know *you* don't want him, but how is he with Ava?"

"Not good. He pays child support, but he's not part of Ava's life in any way."

"What an asshole," Lainey muttered.

"Yeah, and I'm the fool who got pregnant by him. See what I mean? How can Benny *ever* accept that that prick is Ava's dad?"

She agreed it'd be a bitter pill for Benny to swallow.

"But I'm sure over time he'd accept it," she said.

I wished it were that simple.

28

LET'S TALK

BENNY

At the end of February, we left Las Vegas for a series of road games. I was finally getting along with Drew Chidders—well, sort of.

It still sickened me that he'd had sex with Eliza, but I more or less blocked it from my mind. I blocked a lot of things back then. Like how I was still madly in love with Eliza. I questioned if I'd gone too far in breaking things off with her, and I thought about the reasons she'd given me for having not told me about having a baby. And why she'd kept it a secret that she'd fucked Drew.

Were they good reasons?

Were they bad reasons?

I didn't know.

All I knew for sure was that they were *her* reasons. And really, when it came to people and their justifications for doing this or that, who the hell was I to judge?

I'll tell you who I was—I was a guy who'd fucked up too many times to count. And people had still forgiven me.

That was it—I needed to give Eliza that same consideration.

Call me a sucker, or call me a fool, but I wasn't a leave-things-unfinished kind of guy. She'd wanted to tell me something, and I'd cut her off. I owed her a chance to have her say.

That's why I did what I did next—I picked up the freaking phone and called Eliza.

Two rings, and then the sound of her voice, like a salve to my soul.

"Benny?" she said.

I had to smile; she was surprised.

"Hey, yeah, it's me," I replied. "How've you been?"

"Um, I've been okay."

"Good, good, that's good. How's school?"

There was a long pause, and then she sighed. "Benny, why are you calling me? I thought you hated me these days."

That right there fucking stabbed me in the heart.

"I could never hate you, Eliza. Don't even say shit like that."

"It's just that I'm not sure why you're calling. I mean, we haven't spoken to each other since the day you found out about me and…uh, Drew."

I heard the cringe in her voice, a cringe I'd made possible.

"Listen, Eliza, about that." I blew out a breath and ran my hand down my face. "Can we just meet sometime and talk things over?"

"I don't know, Benny. Are you sure you want to see me?"

Hell, yes, because I fucking still love you, I wanted to scream.

Instead, I went with a more innocuous, "Look, I'm not gonna lie.

I miss you like crazy, Eliza. And I don't know if this is what love feels like when someone is no longer in your life, but my whole world feels empty with you not in it. I swear nothing has meaning, goddammit. I go through the motions and I get shit done, but it's all fucking empty."

Silence.

Fuck, I'd gone too far. I shouldn't have brought up the L-word. Any affection Eliza had for me probably died when I ended our relationship.

But then, she said softly, "I still love you, too, Benny."

There was a chance for us!

"Will you meet with me, then?" I implored.

"Yes, I will."

"Oh, thank Christ." I let out one long-ass relieved breath. "I know there was more you wanted to say that day. And I want you to know I'm ready to listen to anything and everything you want to tell me."

"When do you get back, Benny?"

"We have a game tonight against the Kings. We fly back right afterward. But it'll be the middle of the night by the time we touch down in Vegas. Can we meet tomorrow afternoon or evening?"

"Evening would be better," she said. "Ava's been a little under the weather and—"

"Shit, what's wrong with her?" I hadn't meant to interrupt, but I was fucking worried.

But then Eliza assured me, "It's just a cold, Benny. Still, I'd still like to spend the day with her, just to keep an eye on things and make sure she's getting better. If she is, tomorrow night should work out fine for us meeting."

"Sounds good, but if Ava's still feeling crappy, let me know. We can always meet another time. Ava comes first."

"Benny..."

It sounded like she was fighting back tears. What I'd said had touched her. And that was okay since I'd meant every word with every fiber of my being. I cared for Ava, that's why I missed her so much. I wanted to tell Eliza that if we got back together and lasted the long haul, I'd be honored to become Ava's stepfather. I'd adopt her in a heartbeat, if that was okay with Eliza.

I *would* tell her all that when I saw her. And I'd listen to whatever it was she had to say to me.

Like she'd read my mind, she then said, "Benny, when we meet I want to tell you the one thing you still don't know right away. If we're ever going to have any real chance, you need to know everything. And I don't want to wait. No more secrets, right?"

That sounded better than good to me, so I said, "Right."

The only thing I didn't know was something no one seemed to, not even Coach—the identity of Ava's father. That had to be the final secret she wanted to share.

I just wondered who it was.

29

JUST WHEN EVERYTHING LOOKED SO PROMISING

ELIZA

What I'd told Benny was true, Ava wasn't feeling well. It was just a cold, though.

Or so I thought.

That night it turned to something far more serious. Everything happened so quickly that it all became a blur. The day had started off so promising, too. I felt so happy after getting off the phone with Benny.

He still loved me.

And I loved him.

Best of all, there'd soon be no more secrets to impede on that love. I'd share the identity of Ava's father with him right away. And hopefully, he'd find it in his heart to accept who it was.

Drew, meanwhile, had backed way the hell off. There'd been no nasty threats, no smartass calls, just him diligently paying the support we'd agreed on long ago. Perhaps even more amazingly, he started texting here and there, asking about Ava. He only inquired about simple things, like how Ava was doing in general. But it was a start.

I'd even recently upped the ante and texted a picture of her back to him. To which he actually shot back a sincere-sounding, *thanks. She really is adorable.*

I was glad he was taking an interest, no matter how small. I knew I had to keep moving forward, as well. Before my last and final secret was revealed to Benny, I needed to share the truth with my mom and dad. They deserved to know who'd fathered their granddaughter.

My dad was on the road with the team, in LA with Benny, but I couldn't wait. Both my parents needed to know the truth before I told him.

When I explained the situation to my mom and told her it was imperative I talk with her and Dad before the game got underway, she suggested a Skype call.

Smacking my forehead, I proclaimed, "Crap, why didn't I think of that?"

"You have a lot on your mind, honey," she said, "especially with Ava under the weather and all."

"True," I agreed.

Skype wasn't the in-person discussion I'd have preferred, but it was what it was. My mom and I sat together on the sofa, with the laptop in front of us, and called my dad.

With a couple of hours to go before the game, we caught him alone in the locker room. He was reviewing his pre-game speech for the team.

After we exchanged the usual pleasantries, Mom said, "Okay, dear. Eliza wants to tell us something very important. She says it can't wait."

My father knew me so well. He sat down on a bench and straight-up asked, "You're not pregnant again, are you, honey?"

"Dad, no! Absolutely not!"

Both my parents let out collective sighs of relief.

Shaking my head, I said, "This is about Ava."

Dad's brow creased with worry. "Is she still not feeling well? She hasn't gotten any worse, has she?"

Dad was sweet. He loved Ava so much.

That's why I quickly assuaged his concern by stating, "No, no. Ava's much better. I just checked in on her and the fever broke. She even ate a little."

Mom jumped in then. "It's true, dear, Ava's on the mend. Still, Eliza and I discussed it and she made an appointment to see the pediatrician tomorrow morning."

"Excellent idea," Dad proclaimed.

He really did worship Ava, which was evident when he went on to say, "I think that's very prudent, Eliza. It's wise to receive a professional assessment."

I agreed and finally got to the point of the call.

"So Dad, Mom…" I looked from the screen to my mom, and then back again. "I need to level with you about something you deserve to know. But Dad…" I focused on him. "You have to promise not to breathe a word about what I'm about to tell you. Not to anyone. Not yet."

"I'd never do anything like that, sweetheart," he replied, looking hurt.

Oh, but I knew better. Drew was on the team, meaning he was within arm's reach of my father and his wrath.

"Dad, you might," I went on.

"No."

"Yes."

Oh, crap, this is the hard part.

"Dad, Ava's father is someone with the Wolves."

Mom's eyes shot to me, and Dad, in a state of disbelief, said, "What? Ava's father is a player on *my* team?"

I murmured a simple, "Yes."

I imagined Dad running through the player roster. Mom seemed to be doing the same, as she was staring at me with a faraway look in her eyes.

Suddenly, Dad said, "Who is it, Eliza? Just spit it out, damn it."

Oh, hell. "Dad, I'm serious, you can't make a scene. Ava's father and I worked out an agreement long ago, right after Ava was born. There was a paternity test and everything, before we came up with the terms. He wanted to prove she was his, which she is. But he ultimately decided not to be part of Ava's life."

Upon hearing that, my mom gasped. And my dad growled.

"He does pay support," I hurried to say. "But there is a bad part."

Again, Dad grumbled. And Mom frowned.

"What is it, honey?" she asked.

"I had to promise not to reveal that he's Ava's dad."

"Wait, I thought you were going to tell us now?" my mom fretted.

Poor Mom, she thought I'd changed my mind. But I hadn't. I was taking a chance that Drew would flip, but I no longer cared. His threats had ceased, and even if they started back up, I was beginning to view him as a paper tiger. He was all bark and no bite.

Even if I was wrong, I'd finally realized that the people who loved me were my allies. That's why I'd told Lainey. And why my parents—and soon Benny—*needed* to know the full truth.

Taking a deep breath, I assured Mom, "I haven't changed my mind. Too much damage has been done by me keeping secrets. I won't reveal Ava's father to the public, but I'm tired of keeping the truth from the people I love."

"Eliza, who is he?" my dad said tightly, running out of patience.

It was time to reveal the truth.

"Drew Chidders. Drew is Ava's father."

Mom remained calm, but Dad went ballistic.

"That no-good, lying piece of shit has a lot of fucking explaining to do!"

My father was flipped out, as I feared he would.

"I'm going to kill him, Eliza," he went on.

I wasn't above begging. Not for me, but for Ava's sake. "Dad, please, no. Confronting him will only make things worse."

"I didn't say I was going to confront him, Eliza. I said I was going to kill the motherfucker. And I will!"

Oh, boy.

"Honey, calm down," my mother interjected, using her best soothing tone, the one that always worked on Dad.

Thank heavens it worked then.

"All right," he grumbled after a few more choice words for Drew, "I'll not say anything to him. And I won't lay him out. But I sure do plan to make his life miserable when we return to Vegas. Practice is about to get a whole lot harder for that sneaky, lying, no-good—"

"Okay, Dad, I think we get the picture."

I couldn't help but smile. Dad was known for his tough practices, but I had a feeling whatever new drill he had in mind for Drew, it would lay him the fuck out.

We wrapped things up with a promise to talk more about

everything once Dad was home.

After we disconnected, my mom turned to me and, in that knowing mom tone, said, "Is Drew the reason why you and that nice Benjamin boy broke up?"

I had to laugh. Only Mom would think to describe a tatted-up giant of a man as "that nice Benjamin boy."

"Not really, Mom," I replied. "I was keeping too many secrets from him, more than just the part about Drew being Ava's dad. That's what caused him to leave."

"Oh, honey, I'm sorry. Does he know about Drew now?"

"Not yet, but he will soon." I took her hand. "He called me earlier today, and we're meeting tomorrow evening to talk. I think there's a really good chance we can work things out."

She smiled. "That's wonderful, Eliza."

"Yes, it is. I plan to tell him exactly what I just told you and Dad— that Drew is Ava's father." I sighed. "I just hope he takes it better than Dad did."

"I'm sure he will," Mom stated with confidence.

I wasn't nearly so sure, but I hoped she was right.

She got up then to go make a cup of tea. I, meanwhile, decided to check in on Ava.

I found her resting peacefully in her crib. Her fever had not returned, but I decided to stay in her room to be close to her.

I sat down on a love seat next to her crib and dozed off.

I awoke a short while later, though, when I heard Ava breathing funny. That's when things went all to hell.

I checked her and she was burning up. "Mom!" I screamed, panicked. "Please come in here right away. Ava's fever is back and worse than ever."

My mom, in her robe and nightgown, raced into the nursery within seconds. She put her hand on Ava's forehead and cried out, "Oh my God, Eliza. She's burning up."

"I know, I know. We need to get her to the emergency room."

"We do," my mother agreed.

Tears filled my eyes and a lump formed in my throat. *Nothing can happen to Ava.*

"Oh my God, Mom, I'm so scared," I whispered.

I let her gather Ava in her arms, as she was calmer.

My mother took over, which was good since I felt useless. She drove us to the hospital in what had to be record time. Thank God she'd always been excellent in a crisis.

The whole drive to the ER, she tried to reach my dad. But her many calls went straight to voice mail, even though the game in LA had ended long before.

"They must be on their way home," I said.

"Yes, I'm sure they are. But don't worry. Your father will receive those voice mails as soon as he lands. He can just meet us at the hospital."

Mom left no less than thirty messages for Dad, all with the news that Ava was gravely ill.

I left only one—for Benny.

30

I NEVER SAW THAT ONE COMING

BENNY

After the game, which we lost, we started back to Las Vegas on the team jet. I was glad it was a short flight. Not only was I exhausted, but I ended up stuck sitting next to Drew.

I tried to sleep most of the way so I could ignore him. I actually got in a few good Zs, but once we landed I woke up with a start. I had this odd feeling like something was wrong. But I quickly dismissed it.

"Ah, home at last," I murmured as I stretched.

Drew gave me a curt nod. "Yep, here we are."

I wasn't up for more conversation than that, so I pulled out my phone. By the time the plane was taxiing to a stop, I was checking for messages.

I had only one—a voice mail from Eliza.

Fuck, man, I hope she's not having second thoughts about meeting me.

I covertly put the phone up to the ear away from Drew so he wouldn't overhear her message. Although he was busy anyway, adjusting his tie. He must've fallen asleep on the flight back like I had, as he looked disheveled.

I forgot all about annoying Drew when I heard a panicked Eliza. My feeling had been right, something was wrong!

"Oh my God, Benny," Eliza began in her message. "I'm so sorry to bother you, but I need to talk to someone." A pause, then, "No wait, that's not true. I need to talk to *you*. You're the only person who can assure me things are going to be okay and they actually will be." A choked sob broke up her next words. "Ava is sick, way sicker than before. I don't know what's happening, but it's definitely not some stupid cold like we originally thought. Her fever is crazy high and… Benny…oh my God, Benny, I'm so scared. She's just so little—"

All that was left was Eliza sobbing.

At that exact second, Coach ran past me to the front of the plane. "Open the door. Open the goddamn door!" he was yelling.

I knew then he'd gotten the same message, or one like it.

I jumped up from my seat, and as I did, Drew peered over at me curiously. "What's going on, Perry?"

He'd been pretty cool lately, even though I didn't really like him. But with something as serious as this, I didn't have it in me to be a dick and not reply.

"It's Eliza's daughter," I said, to which he really perked up. *Odd.* "Uh, I think you saw her once in the sports complex. Eliza was holding her that day you ran into us."

I glanced up to the front of the plane and noticed Coach was long gone. The door was open and players were starting to jostle to get past me and off the plane.

They had no idea what was going on; they were just tired and wanted to go home.

Drew remained seated, for no good reason I could discern, other than maybe Mr. Dickhead had a soft spot for babies.

What other reason would explain the extremely concerned look on his face? Plus, he'd really wanted to hold Ava that day we ran into him.

His voice cracked ever so slightly when he went on to ask, "What exactly is wrong with Ava?"

Wow, he must really love babies, remembering Eliza's daughter's name and all.

With a sigh, I sat back down next to him, partially to allow the rest of the players to make their way down the aisle unimpeded, but also because I was a little touched by Drew's concern. Maybe he wasn't so awful.

Moved by a side of Drew I'd never seen, I quietly replied, "Ava's really sick. Eliza left me a voice mail about it. She and her mom are taking Ava to the ER. Hell, they're probably there by now. I plan to drive over to the hospital the second we're off this plane."

"I see," Drew murmured.

I gestured to the front of the aisle, where the last of the players were de-planing. "I'm sure that's why Coach bolted out of here in such a big hurry. He's probably already on his way. Speaking of which, I really need to get going."

"No. Wait." Drew twisted in his seat.

"Why?" I inquired as I started to get up. I really wanted out of there. "What do you want?"

Drew blew me away, so much so that I had to sit back down, when he then said, "I want to go with you."

"Huh? You want to go to the hospital?"

"Yes."

I was mind-boggled. What reason could *he* possibly have for wanting to come to check on a little baby?

And then it hit me—was this some sort of sick attempt to make a play for Eliza while she was at her weakest?

Fuck, man, he was way more of a prick than I'd imagined.

"Why in the hell would *you* want to go to the hospital?" I demanded to know.

Leaning forward, he quietly hissed, "Because *I'm* Ava's father, dumbass."

I never saw that one coming.

31

NOW IT'S ALL CLEAR

ELIZA

There comes a time in everyone's life when priorities are made clear. My time was that night at the hospital.

As I was in the waiting room, awaiting word on Ava—the nurses and doctor had shooed me and Mom out of the examining room because we were too upset to stay—I realized two things.

One was obvious—Ava was and always would be my top priority, even above my own self.

And two—this was the new one—I would not only tell Benny everything as planned, but if he chose to run away this time, I would *not* let him go. Unlike before, I wouldn't sit around and wait for him to call. I'd fight for him. That's what you do for the ones you love.

Speaking of which, I got up and went to the nurses' station, where I again asked for information on Ava.

"There's no word yet, Ms. Townsend," a nurse told me. "It shouldn't be much longer, though."

I'd heard that three times now. Groaning in frustration, I returned to the waiting room, where my mom had just returned from the vending machines.

She had coffee, and I said, "I hope it's strong."

Holding out one of those cardboard cups with the playing cards on it, she replied, "It's not Starbucks, but it should keep you awake."

I snorted. "Ha, I couldn't sleep right now if my life depended on it. I just want to stay alert."

"I hear you, honey. I feel the same way."

I took a sip, and Mom, who was holding an already half-empty cup of what looked to be coffee as black as mine, inquired, "Still no word on Ava?"

I shook my head. "No, nothing yet. They keep saying soon."

She sat down. "The waiting's the hardest part."

I plopped down next to her and agreed, "It sure is."

Looking around, she quietly stated, "Hey, I know our phones are supposed to stay off, but I couldn't resist. I checked mine down in the vending area when I was buying the coffee."

"Oh? Any word from Dad?"

"Yes. He's back, and he's on his way here."

I blew out a breath. "Thank God."

She continued to watch me like there was something more she wanted to say, so I asked, "What is it?"

After taking a thoughtful sip of her coffee, she lowered her cup and replied, "Your father's on his way, but you should know something."

"Uh-oh, what now?"

"He's not alone, Eliza."

Huh?

Had Benny received my message and asked to ride with my dad? Yeah, that had to be it. Drew would be the only other option, but him asking to come to the hospital, assuming he even knew what was going on, would be about as likely as hell freezing over.

Still, I figured I'd better check. "Did Dad say if Benny is with him?"

"I don't know, Eliza. Your dad left just the one voice mail. And all he said was what I told you—that he's not alone."

"You should've called him back and asked for details," I murmured, fretting.

"I couldn't, honey. I was already standing in front of a sign that read 'absolutely no cell phones.' I didn't want to push my luck and have someone confiscate my phone."

"Oh, Mom." I rolled my eyes, but assured her, "That's okay. I'm sure Benny is with Dad. I left him a voice mail on the way to the ER, so he knows what's going on."

Benny had clearly gotten that message.

And he was coming through.

He really did care about Ava…and me.

Thank God, because I needed him now more than ever.

Something I especially felt when the doctor who'd examined Ava came around the corner looking somber and grim.

32

AN UNEASY TRUCE

BENNY

"What did you just say?"

Surely, I'd heard Drew wrong.

I guess not since he said again, "I'm Ava's father."

"What the fuck?" I glared at him. "How could that even be? How could something like that happen?"

I was stunned, too stunned to think rationally.

Drew stared at me, shaking his head until I waved him off. "Wait. Don't answer that last part."

He didn't, thank God.

After a minute, during which I composed myself so I wouldn't haul off and punch the prick in the jaw, I said, "So Eliza got pregnant from one of those times you two were together?"

"Yeah," he sighed. "She did."

Now that it was really sinking in, I was angrier than ever. How had I not put two and two together? I guess because I didn't want to.

But where had he been all this time? He'd been in Vegas for weeks now.

"I have a question for you," I ground out between clenched teeth.

"Yeah, what?"

Leaning in close, I growled, "Why the fuck haven't you been in your child's life? Eliza has repeatedly told me that Ava's father has no interest in her. Yet here you are now, telling me you want to go to the hospital with me."

He shuffled in his seat nervously, no doubt feeling put on the spot. Good.

"Speaking of the hospital, we should get going," he said.

"Not until I hear your reason for not caring one shit about your daughter up until five minutes ago."

"I don't have a good reason," he snapped. "I guess I'm just a prick, okay?"

"Clearly," I coughed out.

I got up then, ready to leave. But I had one last thing to say to the asshole. "You can drive your own fucking self to the hospital."

"Fine," he spat, standing as well. He had to slouch since he was in the window seat, and I snickered as I walked away.

It didn't take him long to catch up to me.

"Don't you dare say a word to me," I warned.

"Wasn't planning on it," he snapped from behind me.

We started down the metal staircase that was pulled up to the plane, but I faltered when I noticed Coach T on the tarmac below. Everyone else was long gone, but he was waiting for us.

I stopped on the next to last step, and Drew, trailing closely, almost stumbled into me.

"Keep your fucking distance," I growled as I turned around and pushed him back.

Puffing out his chest, he barked, "Get your hands off me, and move the fuck out of my way so I can go see *my* daughter."

"You motherfucker," I snapped. "I care more about that little girl than you do."

I was about to deck him, but Coach ran over and stepped in, wedging himself between us.

After breaking us apart, he said, "Enough! Both of you need to knock it the fuck off."

Focusing on just me then, he said quietly, "I'm guessing you now know."

Ah, so Coach knows Drew is Ava's father.

"Yes," I replied, sighing. "I know."

"Well, then"—Coach gestured to where the cars were parked—"I think we have someplace we need to be. But I have a problem. I don't trust you two alone for a minute. Therefore, if you two are planning to come to the hospital, *I'll* be the one driving. You'll ride with me."

Coach T gave me and Drew a warning glare not to argue with him, so I just replied, "Okay, thanks."

"Yeah, thank you," Drew murmured.

I was stuck riding with the prick.

That was okay, I'd ignore him.

Before we reached Coach's truck, however, Drew turned to me and stuck out his hand. "How about a truce, Benny?"

I reluctantly agreed, shaking his hand, but not without warning, "This lasts only till we make sure Ava is all right."

"Agreed, dickhead."

33

BACK TOGETHER

ELIZA

Thankfully, it was just his demeanor, the doctor looking somber and grim. He actually had good news—Ava would be fine. She was doing much better already and would recover completely.

"Babies tend to run high fevers when they're sick," he explained. "Nonetheless, it was a wise decision to bring her in. You never know."

"Exactly my thinking," I agreed wholeheartedly.

The doctor then said, "Even though things look excellent, we'd still like to keep Ava overnight for observation."

I wasn't arguing that. "Yes, of course."

Ava would be fine and that was all that mattered. I was so relieved that I almost collapsed. But my ever-steady mom placed her hand on my elbow, keeping me upright.

"You're completely sure she'll be all right?" I double-checked with the doctor. "There'll be no long-term effects from that high of a fever?"

He smiled reassuringly, the first of the night. "Your baby will be fine, Ms. Townsend."

"Thank you, thank you."

My mom echoed my sentiment, and then since we couldn't really hug the doctor, we hugged each other.

When we broke apart, I asked, "When can I see Ava?"

The doctor checked his watch. "Give it about ten more minutes. I'll have a nurse come and get you once she's settled."

My dad rounded the corner just then, and I ran to him.

"Dad, Dad, Ava's going to be fine."

I was about to throw my arms around him, but then I saw who he was with. Benny, which was wonderful, but also, "Drew?"

He nodded curtly. "Hello, Eliza."

"What are you doing here?" I snapped.

"I heard what happened, and I came to check on my child."

Ugh, he just said that in front of Benny.

"You're such an asshole, Drew." I turned to face Benny. "God, this was *not* how you were supposed to find out he's the father. I'm so sorry."

To my surprise, he just shrugged. "Eh, it is what it is."

"Wait, you already know Drew is Ava's father? And you're okay with it?"

"Yes, I know. And I'm not gonna lie, Eliza, I wish it were someone else."

My shoulders slumped as I muttered, "I tried to tell you that night."

"I know." He smiled sadly. "And I cut you off. I know now, though, and that's all that matters."

It seemed too easy, so I said, "Benny, are you absolutely sure you're okay with this? I mean, Drew is Ava's dad. And you *hate* him."

"Hello," Drew interjected. "I'm standing right here."

My father coughed and mumbled that he had something he needed to talk to my mother about. They took off together, and Benny, to his credit, stepped away, as well. Hell, I'd want out of the direct line of fire, too. 'Cause it was about to get ugly...

Poking my finger in Drew's chest, I ground out, "You have some nerve, buddy."

He scoffed, "What the hell is that supposed to mean?"

"It *means* you haven't expressed one iota of interest in your daughter's life. Yet here you are, showing up at the hospital when she's sick, acting all...I don't know." I waved my hand, trying to find the right words. "Fatherly," I spat out, at last.

"I *am* her father, Eliza," he replied tightly. "And as for taking an interest, I've been trying to do that lately."

I let out a snort. "A few texts here and there hardly make you a good dad."

"But, Eliza, I *am* her dad. Good or not, I helped create her."

"Oh, that's just lovely." I threw up my hands. "Finally acknowledging a role in her life, huh?"

"I've been paying you money!"

"And saying all along not to tell anyone you're her dad," I shouted.

"Maybe I've changed my mind about all that. I was wrong about some things, and a little harsh."

"Well, that's new," I mocked.

He shrugged. "I've had time to think since I've been here in Vegas, and what can I say? People change."

"How convenient, Drew."

I choked back a sob and Benny glanced over, brow raised. I knew he'd come to my rescue in an instant.

But this was my fight.

I shook my head, and Drew, noticing my communication with Benny, snapped, "What? You have to confer with Perry on this matter? Well, let me tell you, Eliza. If you think I need *his* fucking permission to be in my daughter's life, you're sadly mistaken. Who is he to you, anyway?"

I wasn't taking Drew's shit, not anymore.

"He's the man I love," I retorted. "Which means his opinion *does* matter. He gets a say in this whether you like it or not."

"Wow." Drew was taken aback. "I thought you two weren't even together anymore."

Hmm, technically we weren't. But I had a feeling we would be soon.

Drew was waiting for an answer, so I went with the truth. "We're working on figuring things out."

"Figuring things out, huh?" He laughed. "Well, it doesn't matter. Neither you nor Benny can keep me from my daughter. I told you before and I'll tell you again, I'll fight for her if I have to."

"So we're back to that, huh?"

"If need be, yes."

I made myself calm down then. I couldn't really keep Drew away from Ava. Nor did I really want to. My little girl was a baby now, but she'd grow up fast enough. She'd need her father in her life. Whatever happened between me and Benny, Drew would always be Ava's biological dad. And here he was, claiming he wanted to be in her life.

If he was being sincere, I couldn't take that away from Ava. Drew in her life, in a positive capacity, would only benefit her. Maybe my daughter would end up with two fathers—two fathers to love and look out for her. In this crazy world, we all needed as many people on our sides as possible. Life was hard.

With that in mind, I said, "Look, Drew, you don't have to fight me to see Ava. I won't forbid you from spending time with her...if that's what you really want."

"It is," he confirmed. "I've been coming around lately, you know that, but tonight really opened my eyes."

He sounded like he was being honest, but I had a warning for him. "This can't be an on-and-off thing. I mean it, Drew. I won't allow you to jerk Ava around. If you're going to be in her life, then it has to be for good."

"Agreed," he was quick to say. "I swear I plan on sticking around, Eliza."

"It's a start," I conceded, sighing. "Still, we'll have a lot to work out."

"I wouldn't expect any less," he replied.

Drew didn't know it, but as far as I was concerned he'd be on probation for a good long time. I didn't trust him. He was going to have to earn that.

Just then a nurse came over to let us know we could finally see Ava.

I held out my hand for Benny. "Join me?"

"Of course," he replied, smiling.

He laced his fingers with mine, while Drew cleared his throat.

I glanced over and saw such pleading in his eyes that I couldn't be mean. I wouldn't lower myself to his level.

"Do you want to come with us, Drew?" I inquired.

He released what sounded like a pent-up breath. "Yes, I'd like that." Glancing from me to Benny, he added, "If that's okay with both of you."

Deferring to Benny was a huge step in the right direction. If we were going to be making decisions about Ava together, we might as well start now.

Benny nodded that Drew could come along, and I squeezed his hand.

I knew then that he and I were back together.

34

THE BEST FOR LAST

BENNY

Over the next thirty-six hours or so, I spent all my time with Eliza and Ava. First at the hospital, where Drew mercifully didn't stay that long, and then at her house.

Coach gave us no grief. He even allowed me to skip practice the day after Ava had come home. I suspected his good mood and easygoingness had to do with his granddaughter getting better. She continued to improve, and soon enough it was like she'd never been ill.

Eliza and I still would've stayed with her into the next night, but her mom insisted we take a break and go out to eat.

"You both need a proper dinner," Mrs. Townsend said when she stepped into the nursery.

We thought she was coming in to bring us sandwiches. That'd been our sustenance the past two days, in between taking turns to shower so

Ava would never be alone.

But Mrs. Townsend had arrived to lay down the law.

"Sandwiches," she scoffed, "you wish. There'll be no more room service at Chez Townsend. You're going out to dinner." She directed her next words to her daughter. "Afterward, go spend the night at Benny's, release some tension."

"Mom!"

"We're all adults here," her mom reminded us. "And you two need some alone time. Plus, frankly, Ava needs a break from you both."

"I guess we could use some time to ourselves," Eliza murmured, looking over at me questioningly.

I replied, "Sure."

Guess we had lots of tension to work off, because we never made it to dinner. Out by my car, before we got in, Eliza came up to me. She stopped by the driver's door and smiled coquettishly.

"What're you doin', babe?" I questioned. "Aren't we going out to dinner?"

"Not just yet." She placed her hands on my chest. "In fact, I say to hell with dinner."

I knew what that meant, and it was all I needed to hear. It'd been far too long since I'd touched Eliza in any sexual way. We'd have to wait until we got to my house for anything too crazy—after all, we were in her parents' driveway—but I sure could kiss the crap out of her.

And that's what I did. My lips crashed down to hers, and I savored and devoured. Eliza was vanilla and sugar and just...Eliza. She was home to me.

"I missed you so much," I breathed against her mouth when we stopped to catch our breath.

"I *need* you right now, Benny."

I felt the same way. We'd just gone through so much, and we craved that connection. We loved one another. And it was time to show it.

It was amazing we made it to my house without pulling over and attacking each other. Eliza was all over me the whole way, running her hand up and down my leg, kissing along my neck, and just generally teasing me mercilessly.

I loved it, though.

I was so fucking hard by the time we entered my house that I just about ripped her clothes off her body. Good thing she helped. It saved her yoga pants and shirt from complete ruin. My shirt, however, became a casualty when Eliza tore it open, sending the buttons flying across the foyer.

"Fuck, yeah," I breathed out.

Eliza was desperate. "I need you in me as soon as possible," she rasped. "I can't wait a minute more. That drive just about killed me."

"I'm right there with you, babe."

Unbuckling my belt, I lowered my pants in record time.

Hoisting her up, I murmured, "Wrap your legs around me, sweetheart."

She did, and I walked her backward to the wall.

"You ready?" I asked when we reached our destination.

She nodded.

"Okay, one sec. I just need to grab a condom," I said.

"No, Benny." She stopped me. "I want to feel *all* of you this time."

Fuck, I almost came right there.

I positioned myself to thrust into her. But first, I checked, "Are you sure?"

I knew she was on birth control, and we'd discussed that we were both clean, but she'd insisted on a condom before.

"I'm sure," she replied.

I loosened my hands on her hips, allowing her to lower herself onto me s-l-o-w-l-y.

"Yes, yes, yes," she chanted as she took me in inch-by-inch.

"Damn," I murmured. "You feel so good."

We stilled for a minute, just savoring the connection, but then I grabbed her ass and took control.

"Oh, Benny," she gasped as I fucked her hard and soft and every which way.

"You like that, eh?"

"Mm-hmm..."

I did a little circle thing with my hips. "What about that?"

"Oh, yes, more of that."

Tipping her pelvis a little more, so that my dick could better stimulate the sensitive bundle of nerves within her, I moved a little faster. "Yes!" she screamed.

When she came apart, it sent me over the edge. "I love you, I love you," I murmured as I filled her.

I thought she'd want to talk afterward, about us and where we stood. But she informed me there was nothing more that needed to be said that we hadn't expressed with our bodies.

"I love you so much, Benny," she said. "And all my secrets are out. You've more than proven yourself. I think we can just figure out the rest as we go."

"That sounds perfect to me," I replied.

And it was.

We were back together.

We were Benny and Eliza, in it for the long run.

And you know what?

That was better than all the chocolate donuts in the world.

EPILOGUE

ELIZA

There were no more major bumps in the road for Benny and me. It was like once I'd finally let go of all my secrets, I was set free. And because of that he and I became a strong and healthy team.

No one dared mess with us, not even Drew.

Surprisingly, the jerk stuck to his word. He became a consistent presence in Ava's life. I'd never grow to be a huge Drew fan, but he in her life was really good for Ava. She liked her dad. Maybe she sensed he was her father, or maybe it was because with her he was a whole different guy, caring and sweet.

"Do you really think Drew's changed?" Benny asked me one afternoon.

It was a month or so into our new arrangement that involved Drew spending time alone with Ava. Benny and I were hanging in his backyard, out by the pool where we'd first messed around.

Smiling at that memory, I leaned back in a lounge chair and got around to answering his question.

"I hope so, Benny. And so long as he keeps doing right by my baby, I'll keep giving him the benefit of the doubt. But let me tell you, if Drew fucks up, even once, this mama bear will be on his ass so fast his head will spin."

Benny laughed and scooted his chair closer to mine. "I don't doubt that. And I'll be right there with you, babe."

"Damn, I love you, Benny."

"I love you more, Eliza."

We linked hands and, positioned as we were, I had to laugh.

"What?" he wanted to know.

Giggling, I replied, "It's just that with the way we're sitting here, hands linked, staring out at the water, we totally look like we're in one of those erectile dysfunction drug ads."

"Babe..." Benny leveled me with a stern look. "Do I need to demonstrate to you that though it may *look* like we're in one of those ads, we are definitely not anything like those couples?" He gestured to his junk, covered by swim trunks but still visibly hard and ready. Just like I liked him.

"Mmm, we sure aren't," I murmured.

He crooked a finger. "C'mere."

I needed no more enticement. I was on his lap, straddling that man, in five seconds flat.

And then he was on me, in me, and all over me.

Ah, life was good.

In the weeks that followed, life got even better.

Nolan, his wrist fully healed, returned to the lineup. Having him back on the first line meant Drew was demoted to the second line. He took it well, so maybe he was really changing. Or maybe he appreciated that Brent, Nolan, and Benny back together meant good things for the team overall.

That's right—the Wolves were kicking ass. They made the playoffs with ease, and winning another Stanley Cup became an even more real possibility.

As much as I loved hockey, I had other things on my mind. Benny had asked me and Ava to move in with him. I'd said yes, of course, and then had gone into full nesting mode.

So there we were, one sweltering afternoon, transporting boxes of my stuff from our cars to his house.

And that's when it hit me—the cutest idea of how we could celebrate the momentous occasion.

"Hey, Benny." I set down a box of clothes I was carrying. "I need to run out for a minute."

"Why's that?"

"I want to pick up something so we can properly celebrate my moving in."

"That sounds nice, Eliza. What did you have in mind?"

Poor guy was carrying a big box, trying to balance it as he spoke. I had no mercy.

Walking past him as I crossed the foyer, I delivered a playful swat to his butt and replied, "Can't say. It's a surprise."

I took off before he could get rid of the box and come after me. Benny had creative ways to get me to talk, though I sure did love succumbing.

With a smile, I left.

When I returned, Benny had all the boxes inside. *Perfect.* I was officially all moved in.

I found him out back, relaxing on one of the chaise lounges by the pool.

He gestured to the bag I was carrying when I called out to him.

"Whatcha got there, babe? Is that the surprise?"

"It sure is," I confirmed as I plopped down on the edge of his chaise lounge.

"Well, let's see what you got."

I began reaching into the bag. "Since champagne was out, for obvious reasons, I chose..." I pulled out a big bakery box. "...the next best thing for celebrating."

Benny's deep green eyes lit up. "Aw, babe. You bought donuts for us to celebrate with? This is perfect."

I tipped the box so he could see the name on the top. "Even better, all of them are chocolate-frosted *and* from your favorite donut shop."

"Damn, girl, I knew there was a reason why I fell in love with you." He patted my ass. "Now let's get our butts inside and pour some nice cold milk to go with these donuts. After that"—he winked—"we'll get down to *really* celebrating."

"I like the way you think, Mr. Perry."

"I know you do," he laughed.

Inside, we poured milk into champagne flutes and placed the donuts on fancy china plates. We toasted to us, smooshing our donuts together before we ate them.

Benny then informed me that he had a surprise for me, too.

"You do?" I said, surprised.

"You bet I do, and I think you're really going to love it."

"I'm sure I will, Benny."

"Oh, I know you will. Anyway, since Ava's with Drew this weekend, I went ahead and finished something for when she comes home."—I loved the way he said *home*—"Do you want to see what I've been up to?"

"Hell, yeah."

"We have to go upstairs."

"Lead the way," I replied.

He took my hand and led me up to the room next to our bedroom. We'd discussed making it Ava's nursery, but first it needed to be painted.

Then again, maybe not, as before Benny even opened the door I could smell fresh paint.

"Hmm, seems someone's been busy," I remarked.

"I sure have. Come in and see how busy I've been."

He opened the door the whole way…and wow. He sure had been busy.

The bedroom was completely ready for Ava, done it up in shades of pink, with all new cream-colored furnishings.

Stepping over to a new crib, I turned to him and said, "I love it. But, wow, when in the world did you find time to do all this?"

Everything looked so amazing, meticulously detailed down to the cute little lambs on the lamps and pillows. Lambs were quickly becoming Ava's favorite animal after Benny had given her a little stuffed "lambie" a few days after we'd gotten back together. She freakin' loved that thing.

Benny went on to inform me, "I painted on the nights you weren't here. And I had the furniture delivered one day when you were out with Ava. Though I have to confess, it wasn't all me. I needed a woman's opinion, so Lainey helped out. She chose most of the decorative stuff."

"What?" I exclaimed. "That sneaky girl never mentioned a thing."

"I swore her to secrecy, that's why."

Lainey was a goofball, and so was Benny, so I had to laugh. "You and Lainey shopping must've been a trip."

"It sure was." He snickered. "You should've seen the looks on the employees' faces when she dragged me into a store called 'Lambs for Little Ones.' The workers got quite the shock."

"Oh, I imagine, what with a professional hockey player coming into their store. How exciting it must've been for them."

"Uh, that wasn't what shocked them."

"Oh?" I raised a brow. "What did?"

With a devious smile, he said, "At Lainey's urging, I decided to have a little fun with the workers."

"Uh-oh."

"Eliza, it was too fucking funny. I told them I was redecorating *my* bedroom and had my heart set on a lamb motif. Lainey went along with it, of course, holding up lamb things and asking me which ones I liked."

"God, Benny, no way."

We shared a good laugh.

And then we shared an even better kiss.

I was so touched by all the work and thought Benny had put into Ava's room.

I didn't know if we'd get married, or if we'd have kids of our own some day, but I had a feeling both of those things would happen.

For right now, though, everything was perfect.

We were a family.

And that was enough.

THE END

Look for Dylan's story, *Caution on Ice*, coming this winter!

ABOUT THE AUTHOR

S.R. Grey is an Amazon Top 100 and a #1 Barnes & Noble Bestselling author. She is the author of the bestselling Boys of Winter hockey romance series, the popular Judge Me Not books, the award-winning Promises series, the Inevitability duology, A Harbour Falls Mystery trilogy, and the steamy Laid Bare series of novellas. Ms. Grey's works have appeared on multiple Amazon Bestseller lists, including the top 100 several times. She's also a #1 Bestselling Author on Barnes & Noble and a Top 100 Bestselling Author on iTunes.

S.R. Grey Facebook:

http://www.facebook.com/SRGrey

Author Website:

http://srgrey.com/

Sign up for S.R. Grey's exclusive-content newsletter:

http://mad.ly/signups/106801/join

S.R. Grey on Twitter:

https://twitter.com/AuthorSRGrey

S.R. Grey Goodreads Author page:

http://www.goodreads.com/author/show/6433082.S_R_Grey

S.R. Grey on Instagram:

http://instagram.com/authorsrgrey#

S.R. Facebook Reading Group (join now for giveaways galore!):

https://www.facebook.com/groups/SRGreyHardAbsandHotBooks/

ACKNOWLEDGEMENTS

Thank you, readers and lovers of this series. Big, huge hockey hugs for everyone, including the amazing bloggers who promote this series and all my other novels. You are amazing and I couldn't do this without you.

Thank you to Christopher John for the stunning cover photo and Najla Qamber for designing book covers that capture the feel of this series so well.

Thank you, Franci N., for beta reading and always providing valuable feedback. I appreciate you beyond words.

Thank you also to Kristin S. and the editing team at Hot Tree Editing.

And last, but not least, thank you to my family and friends, and to my esteemed hockey "consultants."

Y'all make this journey possible.

Here's your chance to read the first chapter of Destiny on Ice, Brent Oliver's story. It's the first novel in the *Boys of Winter* series. Oh, and there's some early-days Benny in there.

GOLDEN BOY GETS A LITTLE TARNISHED

BRENT

My father was a great hockey player. Back in the day, in the era of eighties' big hair and synthesized music, Billy Oliver won not just one, but two Stanley Cups. He was awarded the Conn Smythe trophy both times and has received an assortment of other hardware throughout the years.

He's retired now, but my dad was once a star.

To me, though, he's always just been Dad.

But as his only child, I have a legacy to live up to. I pray I don't disappoint him. I pray someday I'll be as good as he once was. And damn it, I better win a freaking Stanley Cup like he did.

I have no choice, not really. Since the moment my father first laced up hockey skates on my three-year-old little feet, the look of pride on his face told me even then all I needed to know—anything short of being the best will never do.

And guess what?

In many ways, I've become the best at what I do, which is, like my dad, play professional hockey.

I've been good since the start, a natural some say. I don't know about that, but I do know that even before I was drafted—in the first round by the Las Vegas Wolves, an expansion team at the time—I was being called "The Golden Boy" and "The Next One."

These days, three years later, I'm pretty much the poster boy for the NHL. And I have a slew of endorsement deals to prove it.

Lately, though, I've been falling short.

And I really don't know why.

Something is missing for me in the game. Or is it something that's missing in *me*?

I blow out a breath and shake my head.

Things started out so great. Where'd it all go wrong?

I made a name for myself early on. Expansion teams usually struggle for years before posting a winning record. Not so for the Wolves. With me centering what was then a subpar line, I was still able to make us shine. We came out swinging that first season in the league.

BRENT OLIVER SCORES THE GAME-WINNING GOAL IN HIS AND THE WOLVES' FIRST NHL GAME, SETS UP TEAMMATES FOR TWO MORE

One month later, there was this:

THE WOLVES OFF TO A COMPLETELY UNEXPECTED STELLAR START

Then things started to slide.

Those subpar players on my line weren't enough to keep afloat a pretty much overall crappy team, even with me centering. The Wolves' owners and management made the necessary moves—they don't mess around when shit needs to get done.

We picked up a phenomenal winger, Nolan Solvenson. He started to play and things turned around.

DDING SKILLED RIGHT-WINGER NOLAN SOLVENSON TO ROOKIE BRENT OLIVER'S FIRST LINE PROVING TO BE A MASTERFUL MOVE

ON A MID-SEASON WINNING STREAK, THAT SOLVENSON TRADE IS PAYING OFF FOR THE WOLVES!

Another trade made at the deadline gave us Benjamin Perry. A big, strong left-handed winger, he was the final piece to the puzzle. Even with far-from-elite second, third, and fourth lines, it didn't matter. Not with me, Benjamin, and Nolan on the first line. We could *not* be stopped.

Benjamin—or Benny, as he's known to the team—is adept at using his size and muscle to check the hell out of any sorry soul who happens to be matched up against him. He simply wears other players down… and then it's a fucking scorefest. Thanks, in part, to his killer slapshot.

Together with Nolan, a sniper in his own right, we were—and in many ways still are—quite a force to be reckoned with. We destroy teams, though not as much lately. But back then, man, we were racking up so many points that the press branded us the OPS line, as in Special Forces.

THE OPS LINE'S SNIPERS OF OLIVER, PERRY, AND SOLVENSON ELIMINATE THE COMPETITION WITH EASE

THERE'S NOTHING COVERT ABOUT THIS LINE'S SCORING PROWESS

We worked our reputation to our advantage. Trash-talking on the ice and taunting players became our pastimes. We also happened to get a lot of pucks in the net.

Ah, the good old days.

We still trash-talk and taunt, but we aren't as lethal as we once were.

"We just need to get back on track," I murmur to myself. "The season doesn't start for a few more weeks. I'll have my shit together by then."

I better, since I'm the captain of the team. If I go down, we all sink. And that's not fair to anyone, especially not to my linemates, Nolan and Benny. Over the past couple of years they've become my best friends, which is a blessing and a curse. It's a blessing that we play so well together, but it's a curse that we also have a tendency to fuel each other's vices.

God knows this off-season we've become far too focused on partying and women. Like me, my linemates are extremely popular. Hell, let's not mince words—we're gods. In the hockey world, it's good to be a god. Guys want to *be* you and girls want to *do* you. Multiply that all by a hundred if you're not an ogre in the looks department.

And none of us are.

Not to brag—though, I guess I kind of am—but I have the most women falling at my feet. Hell, I've had women who've wanted to *lick* my feet.

Like, literally.

There was this crazy bitch this one time…

Wait, I digress. Back to where our team is today—floundering in a sea of mediocrity.

After that first good regular season, we fell apart during the playoffs. A dirty hit that sent me flying into the boards also sidelined me with a concussion. It didn't end there. More bad luck plagued our team. Nolan went into a scoring slump, and Benny took a punishing check against the boards that broke his foot. We were knocked out of the playoffs in the first round.

I went to Minneapolis, my hometown, to sulk.

"Next year will be different," my always-positive father tried to reassure me.

He was wrong.

We missed the playoffs entirely the following year, for reasons still unknown.

Then there was the season that just ended this past spring—another disappointment.

LAS VEGAS WOLVES FOLD, KNOCKED OUT ONCE AGAIN IN THE FIRST ROUND

Needing a break from all things desert-life, I said to Nolan and Benny, "Fuck this shit."

That was over three months ago. We were in the middle of cleaning out our lockers for the summer. My linemates looked at me, confused.

And then Nolan finally asked, "Fuck what shit, Oliver? What are you going on about over there?"

"Everything," I replied, gesturing around the empty locker room. "We're done, finished. Let's get the hell out of this place for a while."

I meant Las Vegas the city—and I think Nolan was catching my drift—but Benny misunderstood.

"Dude," Benny began, "we *better* get outta here soon." He checked his watch. "We have a tee time at two."

He meant the golf game we had planned, but I was having none of that.

"Fuck golfing," I snapped. "I'm talking about *really* getting out of here. I think we deserve a much-needed break from this whole damn town."

Nolan looked intrigued. "What'd you have in mind?"

I happily shared with him and Benny what I'd been thinking about for days. "Let's head up to my house in Minnesota. We can spend the summer on the lake." I grinned, bad intentions in mind. "You know I'm a fucking rock star up there. We can party every night. Hell, we can fuck and get fucked up till training camp starts up in September."

Benny was in immediately, but Nolan had to think it over in his thoughtful kind of way.

At last, he said, "Okay, let's do it."

Since that day we've been partying like rock stars. Or, more accurately, like out-of-control hockey players.

We're still on a roll, even though it's August and we have to fly back to Vegas real soon. Until then, however, I've vowed my cool contemporary house by the lake will remain *the* place to party. It's our OPS base for debauchery, after all.

In reality, though, this craziness can't go on. We all know that.

Even wild and crazy Benny had the sense to ask me just last week, "Dude, what should we do?"

"About what?"

I was in the midst of texting a local puck bunny to see if she wanted to meet me for a quickie, so I was a bit distracted.

Benny sighed. "We gotta report to camp in a less than a month. Guess it's time to start thinking about slowing down with the girls, the booze, the—"

I put down my phone and cut him off with a raucous, "Hell no, my friend. We just need to scale it back a little."

"Scale it back in what way?" Nolan, who walked in the room just at that moment, wanted to know.

I shrugged. "Maybe have smaller parties? Maybe drink a little less?"

We all agreed to those things, but we haven't followed through. In the past seven days we've abstained from partying for all of two.

This is so not going to play well with the team. My diet is crap, and I'm nowhere near peak playing shape. Sure, my body looks all lean and cut, meaning you'd never know I wasn't ready to hit the ice rearing to go, but looks can be deceiving. I went out for a run just the other day and came back fucking winded as hell.

That was a first.

Still, I'm confident I can get back into playing shape in no time. It's the inside of my head that's kind of a mess. I just don't fucking care about winning, not anymore. I mean, I do, but I don't. Does that make sense?

Nah, it doesn't to me, either. But I better figure it out, and fast.

Where's my drive to get my shit together? Where's my commitment to winning, my obligation to my players?

I ask myself these things every day now, but I guess the answers are clouded by my drinking copious amounts of alcohol and fucking way too many puck bunnies.

Dad would be so proud—not.

Well, he would be glad I diligently use protection. I haven't gone *that* far off the rails. Still, wrapping my dick up isn't enough to keep management off my ass. My agent already informed me—this morning, in fact—that the Wolves' ownership group has a pretty good idea of what I've been up to, along with my teammates, here in Minneapolis.

I listened half-heartedly when my agent woke me up to say, "Don't blow this off, Brent. Management is *not* happy with you. There's a certain image they expect you to uphold, and you're not doing that."

God forbid I'm not the team's "Golden Boy." I'm "The Next One," remember?

Bullshit, it's all crap.

Coach Townsend called me shortly after I got off the phone with my agent. He had the same warning.

"You don't want the team to take action. You're not going to like what they have in store for you, Brent, if you keep up with this bad behavior."

"Oh, come on," I replied, laughing. "The Wolves can't fire me. And what could be worse than that?"

Coach T chuckled like he knew something.

Hmm...

"I can't worry about that shit today," I said to him. "I'll start cleaning up my act tomorrow."

"Brent..." Coach T sounded doubtful.

"Really, I will," I insisted.

That was a few hours ago. And I plan to make some changes. But maybe not quite yet.

"Before tomorrow gets here," I justify to myself, "we still have the rest of today. And that means there's time for one more party."

I stride into the second-floor living room of my house, a spacious and angled space overlooking the huge lake on my property. Peering out at the crystal blue water, I announce to Benny and Nolan, "Listen up, boys. We're having one final blowout tonight, a party to end all parties."

There's a murmur from Nolan, but nothing from Benny.

"We're going to do this one right," I go on. "We party tonight. But then, when tomorrow arrives, we're done with messing around. We start training full-on."

Yeah, right, a little voice in my head coughs out.

I look around since no one besides my guilty conscience seems to be chiming in.

It's early afternoon and the sun is bathing the room—my favorite, by the way, with the way it juts out over the lake showcasing the floor-to-ceiling windows on two sides and a massive deck with a mile-long view on the other—in a warm summer glow.

Nolan, who is lounging on an easy chair with a beer in his hand, raises his bottle. "I'm in," he says.

His words aren't the least bit slurred, even though he's been drinking straight through since last night's bash.

"And then, yeah," he continues, agreeing with me, "we'll start getting ready for camp."

Despite his ability to suck down alcohol like a fish, Nolan hasn't veered too far off course. Getting back on track won't be hard for him. He's like Mr. Discipline. And he's not fooling anyone, anyway. I caught him working out in my basement gym a few days ago. With the way he was pumping iron I suspect he's been training consistently for a few weeks now.

There's still not been a response from Benny, which is unusual. Dude's always up for a party. He's probably the worst of us when it comes to out-of-control antics.

And that's saying a lot.

"Hey, where's Benny?" I ask Nolan as I scan the shadows of the room.

He nods to a sofa that's been pushed way-ass off to a far corner.

"Oh, I should've known." I chuckle as I take in an eyeful.

Benny is sprawled out on a sofa in the shadows, sleeping like a baby. His massive chest is rising and falling in perfect rhythm with the ticking clock on the stone mantel above his head. Some puck bunny he was fucking around with last night is with him, passed out on top of him.

The sheet covering their naked bodies is hiked up just enough to afford a view of the girl's creamy thigh, which is casually slung over my linemate's muscular, hairy-as-hell leg, and positioned under his semi-exposed junk.

Chuckling at Benny's total lack of modesty, I pick up a throw pillow and lob it at his head—the one that clearly controls all his thinking.

And he scores!

As the pillow makes contact—and how could it not with a pole like that marking my target?—the sheet falls off completely. I get a quick flash of perky tits and tiny ass. And then, shit—a big honking piece of man-meat assaults my eyes.

"Dude," I snort, mock-offended. "You need to cover that shit before you blind us all."

Benny stirs to life. Sitting up, he barks, "What the fuck, Oliver? I was having the best dream ever. That is till you started tossing shit at my balls. "

Nolan lets out a low chuckle. "Only you, Benny, could find a way of using 'tossing' and 'balls' in the same sentence. But really"—he tilts his bottle to Benny's dick—"you need to do what Brent said and cover that shit up."

Throughout this entire brain-draining exchange, the girl wakes up. And damn, she looks young. Letting out a little squeak, not unlike a hamster, she gathers the sheet around her naked self and scurries off to where she seems to think the bathroom is.

I only know this 'cause she's muttering something about having to pee. But the poor girl has no idea where to go. Hamster-girl flies past me, heading down the wrong hallway, the one that leads to my bedroom.

As I rush to retrieve her, I can't help but grumble, "Why in the hell do they always think the damn bathroom's down *my* hall?"

I catch up to and redirect the girl, pointing her in the correct direction. "It's that way, sweetheart," I say in my kindest tone.

No need to be an asshole; the poor thing already looks shell-shocked. Though whether that's due to waking up in a strange house or waking up next to that monstrous thing Benny calls a cock, I have no clue.

"Thanks, Mr. Oliver," she replies.

And then she runs off.

"*Mr.* Oliver?" I shake my head. "What the fuck is up with that? If she thinks I'm old and I'm only twenty-two, then…"

Whoa, wait.

Hurrying back out to the living room and pointing an accusatory finger at Benny, I say, "That chick better be over eighteen, dude. We're in enough trouble already with the team."

Benjamin Perry is twenty-eight, but he likes younger girls. Nothing illegal, so don't get your panties in a bunch. He just happens to favor babes who either look young, or are *just* old enough.

"She's twenty-three," he replies, sounding hurt by my accusation.

"What? Five years past eighteen?" Nolan peers over at me and smirks. "Hey, Oliver, you think Benny is working up to go cougar on us?"

Laughing, I reply, "Seeing as he's on his way to fucking the full spectrum of girls in their twenties, I do indeed think he's secretly working his way up to thirty."

"Small steps," Nolan says.

"Fuck you," Benny interjects. "You're both dickheads."

I put up my hands. "Hey, don't be pissed at me. Take it up with Nolan. He started with the jokes. I only brought up the chick's age for your own protection. I'm always looking out for you, buddy."

"Yeah, you usually are," he concedes. "And thanks for that." He shoots me an apologetic grin. "You really are a good kid at heart."

I shrug, feeling a little self-conscious at being called a kid. But then I see what Benny is up to, preparing to bust my balls.

Sure enough, the next words out of his mouth are "You do know I mean *kid* in a good kind of way. Like maybe"—he smirks—"a *golden boy* sort of style."

"Ha. Ha," I retort. And since he's enjoying yanking my chain far too much, I shoot him the bird. "Shut the fuck up, man."

Benny may give me a hard time, but his underlying sentiment is genuine. What he said about me being a good guy, like a decent person, is true. Despite all the craziness of late, I want nothing but the best for my friends. And just because I've been fucking up my own life lately doesn't mean Benny's and Nolan's lives have to go down the shitter too.

Really, I probably should've never invited them to Minnesota. I should have come up to the lake house by myself. That would've been the smart thing to do, especially if my intention all along has been to piss away my career.

I don't really want that, though, do I?

No.

I just need some help in getting back on track.

But where would I find something like that?

Ah, fuck it.

"So what do you say, Benny?" I ask, back to focusing on the party. "You in?"

He stretches, covering his dick with the pillow I threw at him. I make a mental note to have all my furniture *and* their decorative accents, especially the pillows, steam cleaned.

Running his hand through his shaggy, dark blond hair, he says, "Am I in for what?"

"Party tonight," Nolan interjects in his usual no-nonsense tone. "One last blowout, and then Brent here says we're stopping with the bad behavior."

I have to laugh. Nolan is only three years older than me, but it's like he's twenty-five going on forty. He's the voice of reason in our crew.

Well, most of the time.

Not today, though. No, today he agrees to go all-out.

With the party plans full steam ahead, we get on our phones, texting and calling everyone we know.

"Tonight we party hard," I declare when we reconvene in the living room.

"Yeah," Nolan says, holding up a freshly opened bottle of beer.

"You mean hell, yeah," Benny corrects, raising the full shot glass in his hand.

"Hell, yeah," I echo, a beer *and* a shot on the table in front of me. "And just so we're clear," I add. "Tomorrow we give up the booze and the women. Tomorrow we start training for real."

The boys agree, and we drink to our plan.

Yeah, tomorrow we'll do all those things…